KU-033-668

A. Risbridge
C. Risbridger
D. Risbridger

The Third Millennium
Book One : Encounter

Adam Risbridger
Calum Risbridger
Donald Risbridger

The Third Millennium
Book One : Encounter
By
Adam Risbridger
Calum Risbridger
Donald Risbridger

First published in Great Britain by
Aultbea Publishing Limited in 2007

First Edition

Copyright ©
Adam Risbridger
Calum Risbridger
Donald Risbridger
2007

The moral rights of the authors have been asserted in accordance with the Copyright, Designs and Patents Act 1988

ISBN 1-905517-17-3

Illustrated by Adam Risbridger

Cover layout by Lorna Gallagher

Script Publishing

Script Publishing Ltd.
106 Church Street
Inverness
IV1 1EP

The Third Millennium
Book One : Encounter

Adam Risbridger
Calum Risbridger
Donald Risbridger

To our family –
past, present and future...

> "Time is only the hand that joins
> the puzzle together to make who you become;
> your actions are the many different pieces
> that will shape it."
>
> - Adaman

• Adaman •

Prologue

His head ached. He knew the inevitable was about to happen, and he could not avoid it, because he was so heavily sedated that he could no longer control his bodily functions, or even move.

No act of nature would allow for such a thing – it seemed a waste of life. *Someone*, or something, had done this to him. A cold emptiness resided inside his head, and he found his soul in turmoil whenever he went to seek comfort.

Nothing. No one.

He twitched reflexively as another freezing blast of air whistled through the hatch of the aircraft and combed his feet. On his left arm in large, dark letters, was imprinted:

JOHN
NO. 5

He was racked with a sudden headache as a flashback triggered, kick-starting his memory. In silent chaos, he fought with all the energies he could muster to salvage every detail possible.

'You are the only one who can help us,' a voice echoed in his head, distinctly feminine. Why, the pain?

'Be our saviour.' The voice left him. He stopped wriggling in a futile effort to break the straps that clamped him down like a wolf caught in a bear trap. He closed his eyes and tried exhaustedly to forget the pain – at least now, he had something.

'You are the only one who can help us - Be our saviour.'

Who did this motherly voice belong to, and what was it trying to tell him? It mattered little now – escape was impossible. He hesitantly turned his head in the direction of the armoured figure that overlooked him, a searing stab of pain jumping up the side of his neck.

"Who are you?" he tried, his voice weak and unheard because of the roaring engines.

'John' looked towards the face of the soldier, and found himself staring back – the red visor covering the stranger's features reminded him of a sea of blood, from which his pale features stared back at him.

The noise as the blizzards cut into the ship through the unloading hatch played hell with his eardrums. Concentrating hard, he could just hear the smug voice of the pilot responding to a check-up delivered by the figure at John's side.

"The good doctor is going to be pleased," the voice on the radio cackled sinisterly.

Chapter 1
The Time Machine

He did regain consciousness, and slowly, against his own will, he found himself in a small ornate holding cell, the bars ahead denying his escape. Cream tiles were placed in unimaginative patterns all around him, and he began to feel claustrophobic.

John itched the side of his knee, the transparent plastic film underlying the containment suit he had been put in annoying him. What were they trying to do to him? Who was he? Why couldn't he remember anything?

His pulse quickened as he revisited the incident on the aircraft – the memory! Was it still intact? Quickly, he dropped his head, blocked out the small world around him and remembered.

It was still there, taunting him, a single item of his identity that had no purpose in his life in the foreseeable future.

He pulled back his leg and fired it at the bars ahead. Like a roaring piston, it struck the bars with considerable force, but they absorbed the shock and denied him freedom.

He cradled his head in his hands, tears swelling, but restricted.

A patrolling guard, similar to the figure he remembered seeing aboard the aircraft, marched past, his heavy boot-stomps echoing through the prison. He stopped dead in his tracks when the receptor signal on his radio sounded – an incoming call. Without instruction, (perhaps the call was the signal to act) he pivoted around and fingered a key to John's cell. He knew the key would fit his lock – largely due to the fact that he was the only prisoner in the hall.

The clack, as the key did a 180 degree rotation was one of the most stimulating sounds John had ever heard in his horribly short memorable life-span. It said freedom – wherever he was going, it was going to be better than in the cell. Or so he thought.

"Come with me," the guard ordered, and he was surprised to hear that the figure clad in the finger-thick black armour was in fact, a woman. Her voice was rough and amplified through the speakers on her helmet, and she showed no sign of wanting to help him. She led him through a network of halls, each several corridors of prison cells aligned neatly according to the organisation's plans.

"You are not to say anything. You are not to attempt escape. You are to follow orders. Understand?" He nodded uncertainly.

No, he bloody well didn't understand. In fact, his first thoughts when he left the prison network were to retort with a list of insults he had thought up during his capture from...

He watched as the woman lifted her radio and dialled a secure number, her fingers dancing along a buttoned signalling panel.

"Target is secure and en route. Over." She clipped the radio to her belt and it swung lazily at her side.

John found the containment suit, and especially the clear film, restricting his movement. He had to pace along the figure's side like an obedient dog with three legs.

They entered a small hall, at the far corner a sealed door that looked like it had to be braced for nuclear impact. His curious mind, now aching through loneliness, wondered what could be behind those doors, and knew it would undoubtedly determine what was to become of him.

"Follow," the guard ordered as she approached the door. She withdrew a strange device, a pentagonal stone that fitted perfectly into a slot at the top of the door. She extracted a pair of keys from somewhere beneath her armoured suit and passed one to him.

"Insert the key into lock two, and twist on my order." John found his fingers fumbling as he handled the key and did as commanded.

"Twist." Both keys did a half rotation in unison. They were placed far enough apart that no single body could move them both at the one time, possibly for security reasons.

Glowing lights on a panel overhead signalled a successful key insertion and access override. The airlock doors pulled open with great effort.

It revealed a pristine white hexagonal shaped corridor flooded with light. John followed the lead of the woman as she ordered the bunker doors to a close and hastily paced the length of the corridor, as a business person of sorts would do when they found themselves a few minutes late for an important meeting.

"I'm here," the woman he escorted confirmed to a probe on the wall.

"Is the subject intact?" quizzed a female secretary over the secure line. John didn't at all like being referred to as 'the subject.' It left a gut-deep feeling of anxiety in him.

"Yes."

She hauled a small hatch open and they passed through together. She gripped John by the arm, for the first time making physical contact. He felt as if a python had coiled around his arm, threatening to bind tightly if he upset it. It seemed to him this was because she thought his nerve would fail under the sight of the structure ahead, a massive spherical machine covered with neon hieroglyphs and geometric shapes, under examination by many white-clad bodies bearing notebooks and analysis equipment.

"Ah!" the lead scientist exclaimed joyously on their arrival. Two other figures ushered them in – armed guards, with sub-machine guns poised and directed. They looked deadly and inhuman behind their helmets.

"Our company has arrived! History may begin…" John was passed to and fro like a troublesome orphan as the scientists ran physical checks and instructed him on how much an asset good behaviour was to success. *Success to what? Why wouldn't they let him go home?*

He had asked these questions to the point that they had lacked any meaning to himself. After a good many minutes of his life had withered away with the eagerness these people had shown to inspect, teach and command him, he was pressed towards the overshadowing sphere in the centre of the facility. The scientists had dispersed from around him, rallying again in great mobs around high-tech equipment placed in dark corners. Machinery sounded and commands were given, a symphony of different voices being fired across the room.

"Initial sequence underway," one voice informed, as a massive gush of steam shot from the four triangular spikes on the metal globe.

The lead scientist, a man bearing the look of a psychopath and boasting the title of 'Secure Operations Director', or SOD as some people called him (rather suitably), the 'famous' Professor Edward Morgue hurriedly briefed John on the operation in place.

"When the lower shell of the machine is retracted," he explained with erratic hand movements, "you are to enter the complex. There is a central mesh of reinforced aluminium net that you will be hooked into. If the experiment is successful, it will be explained to you what we are attempting," the man lied. Unknown to John, if the experiment was successful, he wouldn't be there to have it explained to him. "It is essential for the greater outcome of investigation XG that this information is withheld from you for the time being. Many thanks, and good luck," he added with a pat on the back in an attempt to make himself likeable.

"I'm not going anywhere until I know –" he protested, but he was drowned out when the lower half of the sphere dropped to the floor, awaiting his placement into its messy grid of a heart. He turned, thoughts of rebellion dancing in his head, but the female guard who had taken him here inclined her head towards the machine and pointed a weapon at him threateningly.

Accepting defeat, and the outcome of his future inside the metallic skull, he stepped inwards, a forest of hands edging him forward. Congratulations were given to him single-mindedly, and he was hooked into the machine. His company departed from the iron skull, the whish of white lab coats the last he would probably see of human life. The lower jaw dropped…

'You are the only one who can help us,' the voice recurred again. *'Be our saviour.'* With mercy it killed him.

Chapter II
The Fera

Three thousand years ago...

The Overcast approached the Temple. As the battle was nearing its final stages, reserve Feran troops were deployed on the battlefield, refilling the ranks of wounded or dead warriors.

Misty veils of absolute darkness suddenly transformed into indescribable masses as they entered the radius of the domed pylons.

Cautious not to wander out of the projected spheres, A'uran and C'kran backed away defensively, preparing for their devastating counter-blow to strike the entities down. It was vital that they felled them during their stray into the bubble that granted them sight of the malevolent spirits.

C'kran tuned in to A'uran's telepathic mind waves – he could sense their urgency, a static that brought the air alive. Caught in his peripheral vision was the image of A'uran activating his cri-bow. A shard of light was suddenly launched from the weapon; the crystalline bolt struck the nearest Overcast and it imploded.

C'kran felt a static burst somewhere behind, and he turned to watch the surface of the bubble ripple as another being breached the safety of the generated sphere. The creature writhed madly, like a ghost composed entirely of snakes, its dragging underbelly manoeuvring it clumsily towards the Feran soldier.

C'kran raised his augmented cleaver and drew it back

– simultaneously the Overcast's serpent head recoiled, ready to strike. The creature, made of electrical pulses ranging from deep purple to black, was invisible until it entered the bubble – as were all Overcast.

C'kran remained frozen, his body tense in the suspense. He dared to make the first move, and he swung his cleaver at the beast resulting in its decapitation. The pulses ran thin as the creature spun confusedly around the bubble, and then decided to flee.

I think that's the last of them, C'kran interpreted through A'uran's receding thoughts.

It seems so, he conjured up in reply. *But we can never be too careful.* He slapped his solar attachment onto his cri-bow. He fired, and watched the flare sail in a graceful arc out of the bubble, into the menace-filled air where the Overcast ruled, waiting for prey to blindly stray into their path. And to them, all prey was blind. They were spirit creatures, and came in all shapes and sizes. It was necessary that hunter teams were frequently sent out to see to their riddance before they could spread.

The flare erupted, casting a light fog that did little to lessen the darkness outside the bubble. That was their terrain. The Fera did not dare venture from the safety they had created. A warning from his comrade suddenly struck C'kran. He lurched forward, now aware of the threat that approached him from behind. As he suspected, there were more Overcast waiting to attack.

The only situation he dreaded had now arisen – he and A'uran would have to face off against an OmniCast, a dreaded slaver of the lesser levels of the evil entities.

The beast lumbered forward, in the form of a large crab. Its pincer cracked over A'uran's head, but he remained still - a hardened combatant never faltered under the psyche of an opponent.

The creature swung its pincer like a club, but it was not fast enough to catch the nimble A'uran off-guard. C'kran found himself wavering on whether he should disperse a few rounds of his cri-bow, but he was always in danger of hitting A'uran, who circled the beast with frightening speed.

Leave it, A'uran ordered whilst skimming the legs off the crustacean with his augmented cleaver. Pulses spouted from the wounds, but the beast remained unperturbed. It wheeled its enormous hide to the point where its head was level with C'kran, who struggled to hold fire.

Don't shoot, A'uran commanded. He was decisive and confident, and did not mind to leave his comrade in sticky situations if he was sure he could intervene in time; a quality that did wonders building on his reputation. C'kran could have killed the beast outright, his itchy-trigger finger hungry, but tamed. If he did though, the MageLord would complain that the kill lacked finesse, that it was a brutal and savage way to fell an opponent. C'kran would be lectured that using tactics comparable with the OmniCast was indecent, and not in the ways of the Fera.

A'uran leapt overhead the beast and swung his cleaver in a single, swift motion, tearing a gash through the creature's thick carapace. The area surrounding the wound then paled until it became a ghastly shadow, the rest of its body a darker form.

Kill was accomplished, A'uran thought, his mental tendrils spreading to allow C'kran to create a reception.

With good grace, C'kran replied. Suddenly the earth shook violently. The OmniCast raised itself, revealing a large gash where its hide had been struck.

Its pincers snapped aggressively, intent on breaking the two warriors. A'uran and C'kran were overcome with revulsion when a massive scaled centipede erupted from its shell and wailed violently, spouting a small black inferno that deteriorated almost as quickly as it had appeared.

The creature extricated itself from its shell and manoeuvred its scaly carapace towards a startled A'uran. The beast's shell was pitch-black, with an eerie purple rim, signifying its density and strength. It moved like a train, its many limbs tapping rhythmically across the cold ground. It veered left and right, circling A'uran until his nerve faltered and he swiped at it with his cleaver. The attack did little to lessen the creature's defences – the blade rebounded with a thud, leaving not a single mark on the creature's scaly length of body.

The centipede rose from the ground, its head peaking and ready to strike. A'uran, with little time left to execute another blow, retreated out of range of the OmniCast. He was headstrong, but not foolhardy.

There was the sound of a blade ripping the air, and an explosion followed by a purple haze as the centipede collapsed to the ground, a six foot spear protruding from its forehead.

Kabang, came the welcome mentality of D'ohk.

Hahahaha, L'gis chortled mentally; his delight could still be felt amongst the wails of the beast as its upper half came crashing to the rocky ground below.

Better late than never, A'uran exclaimed, moving into a defensive stance. The suddenly motionless beast brought uneasiness over him. Omnicasts were renowned for their perseverance and fearsome viciousness. D'ohk leapt upon the fallen Omnicast and removed his spear. No signal of warning was given when the beast exploded, again releasing another being. Taking the form of a winged leviathan, the Omnicast shuddered before spreading its wings, blocking out the sun. Dark purple tints of mist that were expelled from its wing tips wavered in the air. D'ohk was attacked as the Omnicast ruthlessly swung its bony head, casting him out of the protective dome.

D'ohk! A'uran shouted through his mind, hoping that he would receive some sort of response. There was only silence in his ally's mind. He had learned the seriousness of such a feeling.

By now, the Omnicast was more aggravated than ever and propelled itself upwards. Filled with anger and a thirst for vengeance parading through his mind, A'uran quickly sheathed his cleaver and brought his cri-bow into action. Wasting little time on aiming, he fired without restraint at the Omnicast - four shots in total, with three piercing the beast's thigh and the final round searing into its foot. The enemy wavered in the air. The crystalline bolts had almost no effect – the creature's limbs were too solid and reinforced to allow the bolt to reach inside it.

Then, with no warning, it retreated out of the bubble and vanished.

C'kran scowled angrily. Now there was no knowing where it had gone. They would not risk waiting for its return – if it had the chance to heal, it could only make matters worse. Although they would also benefit from its periodic departure, replenishing ammunition and healing minor wounds would make little difference on their next encounter.

D'ohk, A'uran thought aloud. *We must find D'ohk.* Already L'gis and C'kran had departed from the bubble. A'uran hastily caught up with them.

Be very careful, C'kran warned. The dark realm of the OverCast lay ahead. In no time they would be swarmed by the beasts, but they were determined to find their wounded comrade before it was too late. Feran bio-chemistry allowed for a short period before death (when mortally injured) when the body sweated a thick film, first to prevent infection in the hope that they would be found, and secondly to preserve their corpse. If D'ohk had been severely wounded, the process would have begun by now.

There, in the mist, L'gis alerted. They took a few steps forwards, and D'ohk was uncovered. His body had taken a vicious beating, but he remained alive. A'uran could sense the relief amongst his fellow comrades. They discovered that D'ohk was unconscious.

Alright, A'uran thought, taking charge of the situation. *C'kran – take D'ohk to the MageLord immediately. L'gis, you and I shall hunt for the OmniCast.* He could feel C'kran's quiet acceptance and determination – A'uran was confident that he would do all he could to ensure D'ohk would see the light of day once more…

Chapter III
The Magelord

C'kran was careful not to stray from the path of light, a pathway to the Feran Residence quarters where one did not have to exit the safety of the light bubbles throughout the entire journey. The path seemingly travelled far from the quarters themselves, but this was not any concern of his – he had never had any business far from the Residence. D'ohk was feebly aiding their short journey, managing to limp his way along, but relied entirely on C'kran for support. He may be in mortal danger because there was no doubt that the damage inflicted on his muscular body could not simply be shaken off.

That was a close call back there. D'ohk allowed his comrade to listen to his mind.

You did well, C'kran replied truthfully. *You are ambitious and young – far younger than the three of us that will remain if you succumb to you injuries.*

That will not happen. C'kran smiled. That was what he had hoped to hear. They had reached the outer sanctum, the nearest entrance to the Residence via the path of light.

I will fight again, he could hear D'ohk assuring himself as he crafted his entry.

Αχχεσσ Γραντεδ   ψου μαψ εντερ τηε ηολψ ροομ

The lights turned on to show that his entry code had been verified. He could feel D'ohk's consciousness sliding away from him, a warning that he did not have much time left.

Do not worry friend, He is not far away, C'kran assured him. He supported D'ohk through several parallel corridors, until he found the door to the MageLord's quarters.

Ah, C'kran, he could hear one of the guards, a burly figure of a Feran named H'aeke thinking as they approached. *I trust this is a matter of urgency. I will allow you access to the MageLord's quarters immediately.* The burly guard stepped away, and the large crystal doors drifted open on approach. C'kran could feel D'ohk's relief through their mental bond. The doors groaned as they slowly rotated aside revealing the giant sacred figure of the MageLord at the far end of his quarters with a pathway leading up to him. Rows of armed guards were positioned at either side of the pathway, all of whom fixated their watchful gazes on the Feran warriors as they entered the room.

H'aeke lumbered aside towards the door and stood attentively. On either side of the room were two enormous cri-crystals surrounded by stone slabs. Feran hieroglyphs had been inscribed on the looming structures telling the story of their history and the Feran Prophecy of a great fall before the future would show itself.

Limping through the rows of guards, D'ohk stumbled forwards as he slowly succumbed to his injures. With the help of C'kran and his own determination he did not collapse fully in front of his Lord.

The two continued along the pathway before several guards assisted in carrying the wounded D'ohk up to their father.

The once dormant MageLord burst to life and rose upwards, towering over the Feran warriors, awakened by the distressful presence of his two children. His clothing was a mixture of crystal white armour that glistened under the ambient twilight zone being projected from the cri-crystals. Their holy figure was draped in elaborately designed cloth with runes of every shape, colour and form possible to imagine. His armour housed brilliant cyan blue emeralds that shone against his marble-smooth suit. He had an elongated dome shaped helmet covering his head and torso. His skin was greyish-blue in colour with only parts of his hands, forearms and feet visible. His form portrayed an image of great importance, so much so that he created an atmosphere of reverence that shrouded his physical vessel. His very nature showed both mystical and leadership qualities.

MageLord, C'kran addressed his leader before kneeling down whilst still supporting D'ohk with the aid of several stocky guards.

CHILDREN OF THE FERAN RACE, I FORESAW YOUR ARRIVAL, his mighty telepathic voice echoed through the minds of the new arrivals. *C'KRAN...D'OHK*, the MageLord greeted his two youngest children. Strangely, his elder two, A'uran and L'gis were not present. He could feel in their minds that nothing tragic had occurred to either though, and this filled him with a sense of relief.

MageLord... D'ohk used all of his strength to pronounce the holy title of his father before his head tilted forward and he lost consciousness once more.

D'ohk! C'kran called, reacting to his ally's fall, *D'ohk!*

D'ohk remained silent and motionless.

The mighty MageLord strode towards the pair, *STAND ASIDE C'KRAN, LET D'OHK STAND ON HIS OWN TWO FEET.*

C'kran acted instantly, not questioning the MageLord's orders. It was time for the MageLord to demonstrate an act of authority.

Holding out his large claw like hand the room suddenly became illuminated, casting silhouettes on the stone floor. D'ohk's body rose from the ground and hung limp in the air.

AWAKEN, the MageLord called meaningfully. Vibrant

colours took the form of forked lightning and struck D'ohk in the chest. The MageLord's focus was completely on the task at hand. The brightness faded as D'ohk's now active body slowly descended downwards before he balanced himself on the ground. Although this event wasn't new to C'kran, he still watched in awe as the MageLord performed this 'spell' with the same purpose and focus he had come to be associated with. He was seen by the Fera as a perfect being, and the leader of all their ways. Lumbering backwards, he crouched down slowly before sitting on his throne. D'ohk stood in front of him, the injuries from his previous encounter with the OmniCast now absent. C'kran moved over towards D'ohk, relieved by his ally's recovery. Turning towards the MageLord C'kran met his gaze and listened attentively, for the MageLord was about to speak...

Chapter IV
The Water Temple

A'uran turned to face the cold mist. C'kran had done as he had been asked, but he wouldn't have expected anything less of his younger brother. He just hoped D'ohk would survive…

Can you feel it? L'gis asked telepathically.

Yes, A'uran replied. There was a disturbance near, a hundred calls for mercy and help from their people. L'gis reached for the Rune of Hiding, and roughly slapped it against his arm. The rune released a stimulant that dulled the mental link between Fera; being the eldest of his father's children, he had naturally become the most susceptible to the thoughts and feelings of his kin.

A'uran simultaneously reached for his.

No brother, L'gis thought sternly. *I need you to keep your sensitivity up for now. When you have verified the whereabouts of our troubled people, then you may apply the rune.* A'uran did as asked.

The voices clawed at his head – for now he had only a faint idea of his allies' dismay, but that would change when he got closer to them. They were asking for help.

I – it's - , A'uran's head pounded with the pain and fear of the people in dire need of help. There was obviously a large conflict taking place somewhere near.

Think brother, our people are in trouble! L'gis said, quietly encouraging him.

The Water Temple, he responded. *It's under attack!*

We must help them, L'gis demanded and pulled at his

brother's arm.

No, we can't, there are too many! L'gis ignored his brother's pleas and pulled him through the mist. As they climbed the hills, the epic battle came into view.

There – look how many! A'uran freed himself of his brother's grasp and turned to run, to flee the scene so that he could rid the screaming voices from his head. As he broke into a sprint, L'gis withdrew a Rune of Hiding and cast it in his direction – it latched onto his arm like a leech and immediately A'uran collapsed, the voices gone, his head clear.

Move - we have little time! L'gis commanded. A'uran rushed beside him, relieved of the countless psychotic screams that tore at his brain.

They approached the Water Temple, an enormous square-based pyramid that was beginning to fall under the blows of the relentless OverCast. The Temple had been encased in a massive light sphere, the only means the Fera had of seeing their spiritual enemies.

They panted as they neared the battlefield; the ground was thick with blood and hundreds of corpses had been strewn across the grassy plains like seeds.

Whatever happens here, A'uran, if death forces us apart, always know that I have been proud to have you as a brother.

The feeling is mutual, L'gis, A'uran replied appreciatively. He had difficulty masking the fear that clasped his heart, but his brother's remark strengthened his dwindling confidence.

The OverCast never ceased their advance – when one was felled, its place in the endless ranks was filled by two more. The Fera retained their reputations as masters of war, and retaliated with all the brutality that they were renowned for, but they were outnumbered by a thousand-to-one. A'uran and L'gis knew that this spelled death for them both, but they were bound to help their people and the Viscount trapped inside the Temple.

Anything else would be cowardice, and dishonourable.

The bubble gave part even before they entered it – a sign that perhaps the generators were failing under the pressure of the armies in conflict.

Crystals pierced the air like a storm of raindrops in a last attempt to fend off the merciless OverCast.

Al Ta'un, commanding officer of the ranks of Fera defending the Temple bid them over to a small alcove in the Temple wall where the defence was at its heaviest.

A'uran and L'gis darted along the clusters of soldiers, their feet now thick with the blood of their people.

Only when they had closed the gap between them and Ta'un could they interpret his mind-waves, as the stimulant Rune of Hiding offered a restriction prior to a few feet where telepathic signals were allowed entry.

The Viscount wishes to see you inside, he told them as he fired his cri-bow sending many crystalline shards into the advancing enemy ranks. A'uran could feel that L'gis thought their abilities were better used on the battlefield. A'uran himself thought of this invitation as a way to escape the ruthless bloodbath close ahead.

Without further hesitation, the pair entered the gloomy corridors to the centre of the temple. The power, unsurprisingly, was either cut off or, more likely, being completely depleted in the effort of keeping the light sphere active.

Halfway through the network of tunnels they met a Water Temple priest, covered in items of religious significance that dangled and clattered around his wiry frame. His face was aghast, and he wept as he scuttled past them to a definite and bloody end in the hell outside.

Further on they noticed the ranks of infantry, reserve reinforcements only deployed in the gravest of situations. The steely-faced troops paid them no heed as they trudged past in their tight-knit formation.

A weak light played shadows across the dusty walls as they entered the main hall of the temple. Fountains decorated the length of the room, in the shape of beautiful Feran dancers or courageous warriors. The extravagance took a back seat in the midst of war and bloodshed that had befallen the Temple shortly after its partner, the Temple of Fire, had been taken by the OverCast.

The Viscount stood in the centre of the room, his hand etched across his ellipsoidal head. He was a direct clone of the only person whose rule he was to abide by, the MageLord, except he was somewhat smaller and bore the colours of his Temple; blue, white and cyan. Each Temple had a Viscount, except the Temple of Light, which was governed by the leader of the Feran populace - the MageLord himself.

One of the Viscount's many advisors paced the length of the room, a goblet enlaced in his fingers.

You requested to see us, Qai N'ova. Can we be of service? A'uran asked.

Should we not be outside helping our people? L'gis suggested, his desperation getting the better of him.

We are doing all we can, the advisor interrupted. He was a squat and plump figure, and yet the blue robes that shrouded him did little to cover it.

You are darting back and forward with a mind-dulling drink in your hands, L'gis said, clearly agitated. The advisor keeled over, perhaps set unconscious by a stimulant overdose. He hit the ground with a heavy thump. Nobody bothered to tend to him.

The situation outside is grave, A'uran continued. *Perhaps you should consider evacuating your people.*

That idea is seconded, L'gis added. *If we rally our forces at the Temple of Light, perhaps we can stand off against the*

OverCast and succeed. There is still time.

THERE IS ALWAYS TIME, Qai N'ova told them as he fitted himself on his throne of ice. *BUT WHEN WE DWINDLE, WE GIVE THE ENEMY A CHANCE TO REPLENISH THEMSELVES. TELL ME – WHAT BRINGS YOU HERE? DID THE MAGELORD DETECT THE SUFFERING OF MY PEOPLE?*

We went in search of an OmniCast that we had wounded in a previous battle. It severely injured my brother, whom we sent under escort to our father. We decided to continue our search for the beast, to strike it down when it was weak. During our search, we picked up the cries and screams of our people.

I SEE. PERHAPS YOU ARE RIGHT. BUT DO YOU REALLY THINK IT WOULD BE WISE TO ALLOW A FOURTH TEMPLE TO FALL INTO THE HANDS OF OUR ENEMY?

Haven't our people here suffered enough? A'uran asked tactfully.

YOU MAKE IT SOUND AS IF OUR EFFORTS ARE IN VAIN. WE HAVE ALSO INFLICTED ENORMOUS CASUALTIES ON THE OVERCAST.

Perhaps, L'gis argued, *but our people will tire of this conflict in time. Errors will be made that could be catastrophic. If, as you have already said, we have inflicted sufficient casualties on the OverCast, perhaps we should unite under the MageLord for a final stand-off.*

The Viscount chuckled, but they sensed no note of pleasure or amusement in his mind.

'SUFFICIENT' CASUALTIES DO NOT APPLY WHEN FIGHTING THE OVERCAST. WE MUST KILL THEM WHEN GIVEN THE OPPORTUNITY, OR PAY IN BLOOD FOR OUR MISTAKE. YOU KNOW HOW IT IS. WE FIGHT THEM ONCE, AND IF WE ARE LOSING, WE RETREAT IN THE HOPE THAT WE HAVE DONE ENOUGH DAMAGE TO GAIN THE ADVANTAGE IN OUR NEXT ENCOUNTER. THEY COME BACK IN LARGER NUMBERS THAN

BEFORE. THE PROCESS REPEATS ITSELF…

The Temple suddenly rumbled violently. Century-old dust dropped from the ceiling, gathering in heaps on the marble floor. A fountain in the shape of an enchanting Feran woman shuddered and then collapsed to the floor before shattering. The stone head rolled until it hit L'gis' bare foot.

This Temple has already fallen, L'gis stated before turning sharply and bolting along the dark corridors. A'uran followed without hesitation.

The Viscount remained silent as he watched the two of them make their retreat. He understood that he had little power left now to persuade his people. Perhaps it was time for someone else to take the lead…

Stay low and keep moving, L'gis advised as he and his brother raced through the network of corridors. A thunderous growl was spat at them from behind as areas of the roof gave in, crashing down and trapping the Viscount and his advisors inside.

A'uran could smell the air of war ahead, but the stimulants protected him from an excessive mental connection. That ability had become somewhat unnecessary now.

The two brothers broke into the light, the collapsing corridors no longer posing a threat.

Feran warriors came into view; only a fraction of the defence that they had seen on entry remained.

Al Ta'un and a squadron of reserve troops struggled to stop the OverCast from breaching the Temple walls.

Come now, L'gis ordered. Al Ta'un was the first to obey. The experienced commanding officer rallied his troops and followed the two brothers out of the safety of the bubble, where they were forced to make a hasty retreat. Through mental bond, Al Ta'un had already gathered that the Viscount was trapped, and possibly unwilling to leave the battered Temple. For him, his priority was now to get his men to safety. This would be a dark day in the history of the Fera; now the fourth Temple would be taken by their enemies.

We must retreat to the Temple of Light, A'uran told Ta'un as they raced up the hills.

Wait, Ta'un ordered and his small squadron instantly stopped in their tracks.

Not now! L'gis was eager to reach the safety of their largest Temple.

The Water Temple is still to unleash its blow on our enemy. Both brothers were confused at this remark. Ta'un's soldiers stared at the pyramid expectantly. Chutes were raised along the huge marble walls, and a ceaseless gush of water ran down them from openings near the top of the pyramid. The whole operation took only a few seconds. Thousands of OverCast were to be consumed in the oncoming tsunami.

It was good that you told us to retreat, Al Ta'un said gratefully. *Otherwise we would have become a sunken colony of corpses.*

We could not have stayed longer anyway, L'gis said as he watched the OverCast vanish under the massive waves. Seeing them die gave him a strange feeling of satisfaction.

This will reduce their numbers drastically, Al said as he watched the bubble quiver under the watery onslaught.

Perhaps with the troops we have remaining, and those stationed at the Temple of Light, we have a chance of victory, A'uran boasted as he peered over the shoulders of L'gis.

There is always a chance of victory, Ta'un said as he directed his troops ahead.

Their journey was shortened by the absence of OverCast. The thick mist that had once signified their domain was now wispy and thin, even gone in some areas. Perhaps the battle at the Water Temple had deprived the area surrounding it of enemies.

There was still the question of the OmniCast and where it had gone. A'uran longed to see the beast dead, perhaps more than his elder brother L'gis who had his mind caught up in other things, namely their foreseeable conflict with the OverCast, a final showdown at the Temple of Light. He could feel through Ta'un that they had not encountered an OmniCast in the fray at the Temple of Water.

The battle at the Temple of Water was, from the beginning, one-sided. They all knew the possibility that they would face a similar end at the Temple of Light. But even though the OverCast had the advantage of greater numbers, the Fera would be serving under the divine figure, the MageLord.

L'gis kept a close watch on the small battalion that had now formed at the head of their expedition. Fera were gathering fast – perhaps it had finally been accepted that no effort could now save the Water Temple. There was no hope for the ignorant Viscount inside.

Ah. A'uran could feel Ta'un's relief. *We enter the Path of Light.* The group penetrated the translucent domes. L'gis could detect the air of serenity that had befallen on the minds of his kin. For their sakes, he would have to stay alert.

They trudged over the barren grounds, the path ahead of them a glowing beacon that would eventually lead the brothers into the arms of their father.

Those who had suffered wounds in the conflict could afford to ignore them until the journey was over as none were in a critical state.

They kept at a steady pace. It was not long until their destination came into sight. The spectacle that was the Temple triggered a feverous feeling of security. Al Ta'un mentally congratulated his company.

You held out well in the previous battle, my friends. For this,

I will see that you will be highly rewarded. This agitated A'uran. He knew they would get their praise in due time, deservedly and without question. But he felt that now was not the time to be promising anything. The war was not yet over. All present would eventually become engaged in the final stand off against their ageless enemies.

L'gis quickly averted his gaze to his brother. Obviously, he had felt his annoyance and didn't want Al to pick up on it. Was now the time for dampening the spirits of their warriors? He didn't think so.

A'uran quickly masked his thoughts and, as if a veil had been dropped over them, they became invisible to his surrounding allies.

Al leaned forward to enter the insertion code. Immediately the doors to the outer sanctum wheeled open. The weight of loss was a heavy burden on their shoulders.

The company entered...

Chapter V
The Horizon

3000 A.D.

A serene light shone upon him from above. The nightmares had gone, the pain had ceased, and he found himself in complete harmony with body and soul.

"Waken up, sleepy-head," – a voice! A *human* voice! It had been so long…

"Hello?" He blinked, desperate to find the source. The overhead panel lights speared his eyes, and the bland tang of distilled air hung heavy on his tongue.

"Wha – where?" He panted, rising from the stretcher.

He regained focus, and there, a few feet ahead of him she stood– as clear as day. He found himself gawking at her in a trance of wonder and confusion.

Was it all a dream?

"How did I got here?" was the fist question. The nurse frowned concernedly, and then scanned his details on a digital notebook she held against her chest with both arms. She had short, crimson hair, a simple face with soft features and bright green, inquisitive eyes. She tapped a stylus against her purpled-dyed lips, in deep thought.

"You were hidden in the cargo exchange when *The Marvel* linked here a short while ago," she replied earnestly. He blinked hard, his head pounding. He felt slightly nauseous, but unbelievably grateful for the company.

"I'm…. I'm alive."

"Indeed you are. In one piece, too. Most people are when they come here." She smiled whilst staring at him. "So, how do you feel? I can discharge you immediately if you're up to it, but the Captain has requested to see you as soon as you're ready."

Thinking about the question, he glanced around the room – it looked like a small medical silo, the image of the Red Cross fund on each corner of the spotless ward.

"I feel… alive. Who's the Captain? I…."

"The Captain is George Cameron Band. Through his bloodline he has inherited this cruiser and his generation of children will continue to do so for two centuries. He has undeniable experience in the fields of directing and maintaining trade boundaries between space-dwelling freighters such as this one, as demonstrated when the Marvel arrived to exchange shipments a few hours ago."

It hit him like a bullet to the head.

"What? We're in space?" The nurse seemed taken aback.

"You look pretty messed up. Physically, you're intact. Mentally, you're like a jigsaw puzzle in a hurricane. We're aboard the Horizon." He massaged his brow with his hand, and felt a filmy material press against his skin.

"But… Earth. What happened to Earth?"

"Oh nothing," the nurse lied between gritted teeth as she nervously averted her gaze. *No-one must know.* "We've just overpopulated it, so we're looking for a possible… substitute home for a new generation. Presently we're investigating the planet we're orbiting as a candidate – it's called Pharsee." John almost ignored her latter comment, as the knowledge that Earth still existed proved enough for him.

"What's your name?" he asked her with genuine interest.

"Ah, I'm Solara. I see there's little point asking yours," she admitted as she stared at the tattoo on his arm.

He had been dressed in a medical robe, which was surprisingly warm and comfortable. Underneath though, was a strange transparent filmy coating. *Where did I get this?*

He twisted uncomfortably in the film and stared at his left arm, where Solara's eyes were pin-pointing the dark lettering printed on his skin.

JOHN

NO. 5

Was this some kind of symbol to a past life? The tattoo told him that he was someone before all this but… *who?* His mind was blank. So many questions…

"Well, can I give the go-ahead for your meeting?" she asked as she fingered through a handful of patient records that demanded attention.

"Mmm – yes," he decided reluctantly. "I will meet with your Captain. Can you tell me the date?" he asked, the realisation that he was trapped in space teasing his mind.

"Funny you should ask. Yesterday, we celebrated the beginning of the third millennium." She could have just slapped him in the face, or attacked him with a syringe, because it would have had the same effect. He was stunned, his brain attempting to read his memory so he could remember who he was and what he was doing here – this was the future, as much as he hated to admit it, as confused and scared as it made him, as lonely and wretched as it had left him.

The nurse observed him carefully, drawing controlled marks on a check-up digital document she had taken from a nearby filing cabinet.

"I'll discharge you now – don't worry that you have no place to go, the Captain will sort that out." She paced the length of the silo and leaned over a small computer, her fingers tapping the light keys soundlessly.

"The ship A.I. is on its way to pick you up. I'll make

allowances – you can keep the robe, and your dignity – I'm not about to send you out naked, despite how funny it would be."

"Thanks, I think," he replied thoughtlessly, filtering through his brain the importance of what she had told him. Somewhere outside the ward a bell sounded, followed by the voice of (presumably) the Captain's secretary, making important announcements to the far-reaching public outside. It was a funny thing – although he could not tell his exact age, he was an adult, for certain, and yet he sat huddled over the stretcher like a nervous child awaiting punishment, or a dog hiding when it smelled the bath foams heading in its direction.

Those are people outside, he told himself. Not monsters that would tear into him as soon as look at him, but *people.* What am I scared of? He could tell that this sense of withdrawal was relevant to why he was feeling so lonely – if he could break it, he might be able to socially restore himself, as unlikely as it seemed.

He twiddled his thumbs in anticipation, waiting for the arrival of the 'ship A.I.'. His head was such a mess – the very floor at his feet seemed alien to him, as if he did not belong in this place or time.

He waited, and waited, and there was no arrival.

"How long until the –" Solara had her back to him, and she twisted around and smirked in his direction when the white-glazed aluminium doors of the silo spun open. A small levitating object floated inside, twisting and turning until it was face on with John.

"Is this the man who was found in the cargo exchange?" the large white-opal object questioned Solara, its focus still on John.

"Yes Charles – but go easy, he's sensitive right now." The robot buzzed around the air in the silo, drawing the gazes of several by-passers outside, until it ordered the doors shut behind it.

It had two small reflective panels connected at its side, and had a virtual face – a small monitor on which its features were composed of blocky pixels in a simple layout.

"I always go easy," the floating robot replied in a self-important manner, its manufactured voice lacking emotion.

Solara rolled her eyes before turning back to the registration computer and busying herself again.

"Follow me, human," Charles ordered as he prepared to depart.

"Call me John," he advised. "I think I prefer that."

"Ok, John. Time to go – follow my lead." John bode Solara farewell – he hoped he would see her again sometime, but at the present he had to get some things sorted, namely where he was going to stay and *what was going on.*

The silo doors opened and closed at Charles' command, and John was led into a wide hall, where traders, scientists, teachers, police, crew and civilians were engaged in the bustle of everyday life. It was an astounding sight – people dressed in mosaic robes in varying bright colours and subtle hues, taking his breath away. There was a prosperous civilisation aboard the Horizon, as he recalled Solara calling it. He wondered how big the space cruiser actually was, and was curious enough to ask his companion who wordlessly guided him through the hall.

"Can you tell me a bit about this … ship?" he asked wondrously as they passed a series of boards littered with adverts on weapons, clothes, furniture, even robotic assistants such as Charles to help around the house.

"Can I buy one of you?" he asked next. He continued to question his robotic guide as he took in new sights. After a short pause Charles answered him.

"Firstly, this is the Horizon, one of the largest and most

recent space launch projects released from Earth. It is of considerable size, and can accelerate on the verge of light speed. Secondly – gosh no! I am not your common pick-me-up housemate, John. I am a one-of-a-kind maintenance and pilot intelligence, archived with the entire Horizon's back memory. I have the most advanced and modern robotic neural frame ever constructed. Thirdly, yes, I know where I'm going…"

After crossing through many halls, Charles directed John through a small corridor and onto a glowing circular panel. John's head was already spinning; he was observing more with a higher awareness than he could hack. It was no great surprise then, that he felt worse when he was lifted into the air by a pressurised gust of air and dropped onto his feet, where he found himself on the Captain's bridge.

"Pickup successful, Captain," Charles declared high-spiritedly and he moved to the Captain's desk. A polished wooden plaque sat neatly aligned with the few other items the Captain was browsing over before he noticed the company.

"Oh John – you weren't due here for another five minutes yet, but that won't be a problem – please, make yourself at home," George offered. He was largely built, and had a face so grim that it looked as if it had been carved from stone. He ran his hands over his greying moustache, as he discarded various items into the bin at his feet.

"I'm sorry things are in such a state," he continued politely, "it's most unusual, these circumstances. We found you frozen amongst the cargo that was being transferred aboard this cruiser, as I'm sure has been explained to you. Flu symptoms and headaches are common after freeze-travel," he reassured John as he drained a great amount of fluid from a metal flask he kept in a drawer on his desk. He clicked his fingers to an attendant who was patiently waiting for requests.

"Make John comfortable," he ordered and the attendant

immediately obeyed, dropping a self-inflating sofa several paces from where George sat, eager to begin. John thought mildly of what he could have done to deserve attention such as this lavished upon him. For all the Captain knew, he could have been a tramp or a criminal hitching a free ride from the Marvel aboard here. He could see in the Captain's eyes that he thought there was more to this than could be gleaned from face value alone, though, and was pleased to find that, perhaps being the most important figure aboard the cruiser, he looked deeply into strange matters such as these.

The sofa unfolded from the small cube it had been stacked into, and he was amazed to see that in a matter of minutes it had expanded to twenty times the size it had begun as. Glad of somewhere to put his feet up, he sat down happily, awaiting the inevitable barrage of questions.

"So, to begin with – this conversation is being recorded by the way – you can never be too safe," he explained.

"I agree," John added hastily. He stretched his legs and nestled into an airy patch on the sofa, the attendant returning to his post, awaiting further instruction.

"To begin with," the Captain repeated, "you have informed the staff at the medical silo that you have no memory of previous events whatsoever. That is saying, no recollection of what happened before your freeze-journey, or why you were in the Marvel's cargo bays anyway?" He ruffled his hair and licked his lips, ready to proceed further after John had verified these statements.

"That is true." Charles linked up into the digital mainframe of the Horizon, monitoring events and doing stock check-ups etc. Every now and again he asked about operations in progress aboard the cruiser. The interview lasted a good half hour, the Captain absorbing every word from John's scarred mind. When he leaned backwards in his seat, passing the recordings to his attendants for safe-keeping, John took a deep breath – it was over, and it had left him drained.

• The Horizon •

"Thank you for your time, John. This must be very difficult for you. I'm sorry but I must dismiss you, I'm overrun with important duties, and well, it's very hectic right now. I will try to make your new living arrangements here as comfortable as possible, and make sure you get any necessary post deliveries from my secretary until we get things sorted out. I've kept you in an apartment on the first floor to make sure you don't get lost. Here's your room card," he said as he handed John a small tag, "and a forged identity and job listing to make sure no-one asks any questions. I'll see that any queries you may have are answered at once and sent to the work station in your flat. That will be all for now. You may be called up later if we wish to run further checks. You must receive a lie detector test for final confirmation of your statement to tie up any loose ends, which will be held –" John heard the buzzing drone as the Captain's earpiece vibrated to signal an incoming call. "Filter those, Elaine, until I'm done here. Yes. Yes." He took his hand away from the device and finished with John. "All further details will be e-mailed to you soon. Your room card has a built in map to ensure you reach your apartment without too much trouble. It was good meeting you. Goodbye."

"Thank you," John replied politely, tired of talking. He just wanted to collapse somewhere he could stay for more than an hour. The attendant rushed behind him to collect the inflatable sofa and disappeared at the back of the Captain's bridge.

Once he had dropped down the air lift, the Captain linked up a secure channel to Charles.

"This is not good," he muttered as he rubbed his brow with his thumb and forefinger. "The results, they…" Charles sounded a tone in understanding.

"The test results display a mutated gene inside him, Captain."

"You mean he's got a genetic deformity?"

"Correct. There's something wrong with him internally, but we can't see it yet. This is most likely a direct result of radioactive substance in the freeze log he was found in. Samples of the material were taken by Professor Edward Morgue, who was recently recruited aboard this ship from the Marvel. The Professor is supposed to be very good at dealing with strange happenings. He's going to send his test results direct to me ASAP."

"Direct a copy of these results when you've got them to my work bank immediately. I want to keep a closed lid on this 'John' character until we know what we're dealing with. Make sure he doesn't stray too far from his apartment."

"I'll see to it that all patrolling officers are instructed on this, Captain."

"You do that."

Chapter VI
Crisis

John found his room in a small corridor aside a Mess Hall, a large area open to traders which was occasionally cleared for special public events.

He cleared his throat, purely out of habit, and examined the small tablet aligned with his room number. Uncertainly, he ran his apartment card through a suggestive slot and it recorded his false identity, on specific instruction from the Captain. The door pulled open automatically, its heavy weight making it almost irreplaceable by man-power alone. He shuffled inside, eager to dress into something more suitable. The clear plastic layer of film around him felt like it had been with him since birth – whenever that was - and he wasn't going to miss it. He instinctively headed for the bathroom.

Striding towards the shower, he discarded his clothes along the way, leaving a trail of white-medical silk and film behind. Never could the experience of washing himself have been so invigorating – with his new cleanliness it felt as if a great weight had been taken from his shoulders. Once he had dressed, choosing a plain and indistinguishable shack of clothes he had found in a closet nearby, he threw himself onto his bed, and after scoffing a few mouthfuls of the nearest wholesome food in the freeze-cabinet, fell into a deep sleep.

● ● ●

He awoke, an appetite for discovery forcing him to get out and about. He lifted his head and prepared to set out to uncover the many mysteries onboard his new home. He exited his room, taking care to lock it on the way out – although he had little in the way of influence aboard this cruiser, he knew he still had responsibility – *start in small places*. He ran his fingers over his bald head and began down the corridor and into the Mess Hall.

His bland robes, he soon found, made him look poorly – they swamped him, for starters, but travelling in style wasn't a necessity to him at that moment in time. He had misjudged the fashion sense of the moving public, and soon found his garments similar to the people know as the 'peasants' of the ship; he appeared as the modern-day equivalent of a ragamuffin. He was subjected to many distasteful and venomous comments, but he continued onwards in an effort to ignore them.

He had no idea that a lack of basic essentials such as money had anything to do with judgement of character.

He wandered into the Mess Hall, wishing to check the prices of the products offered for sale by the traders. And there again, were their stereotypic stares – a dismissive glance drove him away from many of the stalls, and even though he knew he was poorer than the clothing showed, he was sure of his ability to be a hard worker – something overlooked in this day and age.

"Can I interest you in some berries, mate?" a small Irish barrel of a man said as he caressed the fine leather of his purple blazer. He didn't seem to be discouraged by John's clothing. "Imported from Earth via shipment of the Marvel, they were."

After observing John's disinterested expression with great hurt, he continued the bribe. "Have you no idea how much of a rarity these things have become recently? Less berries on Earth now than diamonds, they say." He plainly had no idea of how little John cared. John uncovered a part of himself that was distrustful of anything that came out of the mouth of an independent salesperson.

"I think I'll pass," he offered as a mild turndown. The man grunted, and his face twisted displeasingly, as if a foul smell had crept up his nostrils. He turned sharply and intercepted another passenger on her way through the hall, trying exceedingly hard to palm off the fruits for a ridiculous price, judged only by the customer's shocked expression. John felt a heavy armoured hand softly grip his shoulder, and he turned, hoping that this was not another trader beckoning his attention. It turned out that this person was a law enforcer – patrolling the Hall as it seemed, perhaps searching for some bargains while he was on duty.

"Excuse me sir," he said lightly. "Are you Jake Barrows?" John briefly recalled the name on his false identity, and nodded naturally. "You have an appointment with the Captain's council to do a lie-detector inspection. He would like to see the results as they come through, so it will be held short of ten minutes on his bridge. You are to go there immediately so as to arrive in good time, which is always appreciated," he said as he leaned forward and winked, "and if you're not sure of the way I'm here to help you."

John decided he'd get there alone.

"Thanks, but I'm pretty sure I know where to go. It was only a few hours since I met with him anyway."

"Well, I'll be around should you decide you need any help," the officer said assuredly, smoothing the stubble of his chin with gloved fingers. He set off in another direction, heading towards a stall selling high-grade license-only weaponry, no doubt keeping a close eye on other happenings as he did so.

● ● ●

John found himself sitting comfortably in the sofa once more, facing the Captain and the test analysers. Several plasters had been placed around his head and arms, measuring any blips in his sweat process.

The 'interview' – it felt more like an interrogation – lasted just outside twenty minutes. The Captain leaned back in his amply padded chair, his arms casually folded behind his head. He didn't look like the type of person that got enough time to exercise, as shown by the appearance of several large chins when he cradled his head, and John couldn't blame him; thousands of people counted on him and Charles so life on the cruiser could continue as normal. The absence of the Captain would be catastrophic, especially at a time such as this when trade of vital supplies was taking place.

"Everything in your statement was, as confirmed by the lie detector, completely true, John. It would seem that a great deal of mystery lies in your past – a shame, I bet you, and something very troublesome to live with." John sighed, relieved. At least now they knew that he wasn't some scheming liar – he did live in extraordinary circumstances, and now he could be credited for doing so.

"We're done now, so you can return to your apartment. Besides that, is there anything you need? Are you settling in ok?" John noted that when George asked him these questions he seemed to honestly care.

"Everything is fine," he replied gratefully. "As far as my room is concerned." With that, he picked himself up from the sofa, and paced thoughtfully toward the airlift. On his first day, he found that he was already exhausted– endless questions, poking into the deepest recesses of his crippled mind.

There was a panicked moment when his breathing was cut short, and the bridge was plucked from beneath his feet, leaving him to collapse in confusion and fright.

Screams from all around were in direct competition with the many explosions in the lower decks. Once he had regained his balance, he stared through the transparent upper sphere of the ship, into the darkness of the void. Tiny lights moved together in space, at the side of the massive Horizon, and he recognised them as engine lights similar to those he had seen once before in an advert on his way here.

George shouted at his advisers, and began frantically making calls as he and Charles wrestled with the problem. *What now?*

John's first instinct was to escape to his room, where he could remain hidden. A sudden urge drove him to seek weaponry, in an attempt to rebel against whoever was evil enough to attack a cruiser with such a large population.

He dived towards the airlift, and found it blocked as the solid physique of an armoured giant hulked upwards, knocking him flat without restraint.

He was quickly surrounded by several more. John recognised them as terrorists, and noticed with dread that they had come well equipped – each one had its own monstrously thick hide of reinforced armour. The aluminium plating shone under the light of the stars which penetrated the Horizon's glassy upper hemisphere. He noticed spatters of blood gleaming in areas, especially around the arm and chest. How many people had they killed?

Their figurehead pressed through the small crowd, a man bearing minor differences from the rest, in that he had a helmet in the shape of a lion's head and his armour was obviously of great age, perhaps an artefact from their heretical tribes.

His scarred and chalk-white face grimaced as he stepped forward towards the Captain, who sat, the phone still buzzing in his ear.

The Captain discarded the tele-clip and handed it to one

of his trembling attendants, who dared only move a few feet nearer him before backing into the shadows once more.

"Who are you, and what the hell gives you the right to attack my ship?" the Captain managed, his voice quivering with anger as he watched on the surveillance cameras Charles had raised alarmingly the blood of innocent passengers spill before these corrupt murderers. The leader of the terrorists stood several feet higher than George, who, unflinching, barked at him like an angry dog.

John witnessed the murder of many passengers on the cameras– as he watched, a troop of guards were being mown down by laser fire from pulse rifles which the terrorists had issued without limit for the offensive.

The Captain looked sick – his cruiser was under siege, and he knew that people only attempted something such as this when they wanted to plunder everything in their sights – to bleed the Horizon dry, without remorse.

"Kill me," he dared, "for I do not deal with terrorists," George stated unflinchingly.

"It is in your best interests that you co-operate, Captain," the terrorist figurehead declared, as a slender woman, recognisably in her early-twenties, was thrown into his arms, her throat level with a glinting combat knife. The fabric of her decorative headdress was ripped and torn.

George shouted rebelliously, unsure of whether to act or try to force the connection to his daughter deep into his mind; to see her as any other civilian – just one of the masses. The technique, as he stared into Catriona's pleading eyes, failed.

"Please," the Captain said, eyes tightly clamped shut so as to protect himself from the horrific scene. "Leave Catriona – she's not the one you want."

"I'll be the judge of that," the cult leader answered disinterestedly. "But, meanwhile, if you wish to sleep knowing she's alive, you'll do as I say."

"Why should I take your word?"

The terrorist leader smirked.

"Because it's all you've got." There was a silence, the stillness in the air broken only by the screams from the lower decks. George was aware that every dwindling second cost several more lives. The price they were making him pay was more than any one man could afford.

"Ok, Ok, tell us what you want – just leave Catriona out of this!" The Captain pleaded as he clasped his hands in silent prayer. A wry smile stretched the length of the cult leader's face.

"I'm glad you have seen sense, Captain. The Horizon's funds – I want them downloaded into the Dark Sun's account - everything, within the hour."

John recognised this as the typical type of terrorist behaviour. Tender was all they cared for, so they could buy large amounts of forbidden weapons to threaten colonies into subjugation.

Charles initiated the order.

Within a second, two metallic flat plates of the flooring rapidly unfolded until they stood five feet high, gun barrels protruding from their sides and readying to fire. Before the terrorists could react, even before the combat knife dwindling above Catriona's throat could make its mark, the sentries discharged their lethal payload – blinding streaks of brilliant light shot across the command bridge and struck down four of the enemy, their bodies amassing on the ground like charred dominoes. John tasted something like sulphur in the air, and gazed, disturbed, at the massive burning holes in the mound of corpses within touching distance. Charles issued the sentries to continue fire.

A path of light paved its way across the sentries' weapons.

The terrorist figurehead stumbled backwards as the Captain silently prayed his daughter would escape to safety, and not be struck by a stray bolt. There was an exchange of fire from both sides resulting in the mortal injury of a navigator beside the Captain and the terrorist figurehead being left with only two companions. Before Charles's sentries could fire again, the terrorist leader had disembarked from the bridge with his bodyguard duo, taking with them John and Catriona as bargaining chips for later.

John watched in fear as he was forcibly taken to meet up with a loose band of Dark Sun terrorist foot-soldiers.

"Prepare a shuttle for my departure down to the planet's surface," the figurehead demanded to a rag-tag group of mercenaries who had finished plundering supplies from a Mess Hall.

"Shuttle 14-A is waiting in docking bay 5, Ridley," one of his more observant goons informed him. His bodyguards gripped John and Catriona, and hauled them along an endless succession of corridors and halls where people still ran, screaming and terrified.

John looked onwards with dread, watching as the terrorists clamped augmented arms around many of the innocent citizens, all of whom were just ordinary people, and snatched them away back into the shadows with them. A sharp stab of revulsion encouraged him to try and break free, but his efforts were in vain.

Catriona seemed oddly composed considering the gravity of the situation, and this was largely due to the fact that she was shocked into silence – the blade still rested threateningly under her throat while there were rebellious onlookers to intimidate, namely the Horizon's law enforcers.

The terrorist hijacking fleet came into view – massive bloated vessels gathered in rows where they had penetrated the Horizon's hull.

Prisoners were thrown into the terrorist vessels. Many had been given enough 'encouragement' to stop them opposing the will of Ridley. The figurehead guided the whole operation with a look of glee set on his face – was this some mission of vengeance, and if not, why did he look so pleased at the hurt of others?

With a clear hand gesture, the last of the prisoners were loaded on board. John, who had been mistakenly thought of as important by the terrorists when found in the company of the Captain, was taken with Catriona and suitably restrained with wires on a private shuttle belonging to the terrorist commander.

He was relieved that they had thought him to be someone he was not – he didn't even fully understand who he was himself, and yet they foolishly assumed he could be of use to them – when he was of no real importance. He was sure they would just toe him along with the other commoners when they found this out, though.

The vessel undocked, thunderously tearing itself from the Horizon's hull, and arced on a guided path down towards the mysterious planet Pharsee.

Chapter VII
Catriona

John aspired to a state of awareness after his restless sleep during the long journey the terrorist ship made in orbit. He stared candidly at Catriona, who had been tied in a tight bundle opposite him. The small enclosure they were trapped in rocked and bumped as the vessel prepared for landing.

Catriona jittered and woke when they made impact on the alien soil – Pharsee. She silently prayed that the humans on this planet had enough clout to repel their terrorist captors should they choose to attack any of the settlements. She knew that was unlikely, as human villages were scarce, except in the Far East where humanity had managed to establish a foothold.

All she had now, it seemed, was this stranger who watched her in quiet contemplation.

"Who are you?" she croaked. She shook her head and the ornate headdress she wore dropped to her knees. She was striking – maybe not considered attractive, but John found her distinguishing bright amber eyes, possibly changed cosmetically, alluring. She had a shoulder length sweep of deep golden hair and a bright complexion, even in the poor lighting.

He considered her question. He was going to have to get used to being asked this. Should he respond, as the Captain had told him, *Jake Barrows?* Did he still have to support his false identity here, away from the civilisation it was meant for? He knew she would probably consider him insane had he answered, 'I'm not sure,' or 'John, I think.' First impressions were lasting impressions.

"I'm John," he replied with great effort. "You're the Captain's daughter, are you not?"

"Yes." There was an awkward silence. "I think we've landed," she continued.

"What do you think they're going to do with us?"

"Use us for bribes, probably – it's their way." She tried to shrug but found herself too tightly bound. "I don't think they'll kill us anyhow – or the passengers they took. It seems pointless to take so many of them down here if they plan to massacre them." Her voice was long, deep and drawn because of the constraints around her neck.

John sighed, disappointedly – why did it all have to turn out like this? If he had just stayed in his room, perhaps, just *perhaps,* he could still be up there in safety. Now he was imprisoned, and at the will of mass murders. A fine start to a new beginning to his life.

He wriggled around exhaustingly, but he couldn't loosen the wires and found that he was securely stuck into place. As was Catriona, who watched him silently.

"There's little point," she assured him a moment later. He continued to wrestle.

"I'd rather not be waiting helplessly when they come to get us." He clenched his teeth as his limbs burned under the wire.

"You know, you remind me of someone – I can't quite place who… but there is definitely a resemblance." Catriona's bright eyes contrasted sharply with the dark surroundings, and John became unnerved under her gaze. In truth, it was actually quite frightening. He gave up trying to fight his way out of the wire.

"Ok, so do you have a better idea?" he asked irritably when the flicker of a triumphant smile darted across her face.

"Be quiet and sit tight."

"Is that an order?" He asked Catriona, adopting a respectful tone towards the Captain's daughter. He recalled how much generosity her father had shown him, before *they* had attacked.

"No – it's advice." They sat in silence for another moment, wondering what was to become of them. Catriona could rest with the utmost certainty of her wellbeing, even amongst the hands of people like these – she was too valuable to their cause for them to dare hurt her. John didn't have that luxury– if they discovered that he had no links to anyone aboard the Horizon, he wasn't likely to receive the same kind of hospitality he did now.

"Yeah, well it's all good for you," John said hesitantly. Catriona looked puzzled as she fitfully tried to move a stray stand of hair which was dangling precariously close to her eye. "You being the Captain's daughter and everything – you've got your life set out on a plate!" Catriona managed to get the strand nestled in amongst her short river of fine hair. She gave John a look of utter contempt.

"Oh, yes, and this whole hijacking thing was so scheduled to happen!" she shouted sarcastically.

"Keep your voice down – what happened to be quiet and sit tight?" He took note that she had moved across the steel flooring several times now. She seemed discontented with her surroundings.

The noise of heavy metal doors being pulled apart from somewhere outside caught their attention. He gazed around the room and noticed a shutter on one of the steel walls. Shuffling uncomfortably, he managed to edge his way over to it. Leaning on his back, he unhinged it with his leather shoe.

Rays of white light poured in on them, and the voices became much clearer. He pulled himself onto his knees to look through – in the brightness he had trouble defining any of the characters outside. He finally recognised one as Ridley, the infamous Dark Sun clan leader who had recently spearheaded the raid on the Horizon.

"What's going on out there?" Catriona asked eagerly. John peered further into the morning light. Strange alien forestry surrounded the gathered figures as they herded prisoners out of sight, so doing with an air of supremacy. What were they doing to them?

"John? I said what are they doing?"

"I – I..." he watched guardedly as the terrorist figures departed from the scene, in line after the restrained human guinea-pigs they had gathered. "I don't know Catriona, but let's just pray we never have to find out."

Chapter VIII
One of a Kind

Sergeant Baker signalled his men to form a defensive formation around the entrance to docking bay 9. Sweat trickled down the length of his face as he prepared to open the door. Letting out a quiet breath he paced the room to reach the controls of the door at the other side. This was the third bay that he and his squad had been ordered to check for any other immediate threats. Charles had made it clear that there was to be no more surprises that could have been easily prevented if correct precautions had been taken. The terrorists were no exception. The loud beeps of the control panel echoed through the corridor he and his squad had recently come through. As he pressed the final key a series of other more distinguishable beeps confirmed clearance to enter docking bay 9. His instincts didn't help his nerve as he sidled against the wall waiting for the inevitable. The moment of silence was broken as the doors hissed before sliding open with relative ease. He peered inside.

The room's lights were off.

Disabled? Faulty? Or perhaps vandalised, as after all this was a notorious hideout for gangs. He tried to reassure himself.

Returning his gaze back to his squad he signalled for the 'move towards me'. His fellow troops advanced slowly. Cautiously.

As he crept inwards into the pitch black docking bay he was inadvertently cast backwards and flung to the floor. Slamming off the hard metallic ground his heart thudded like a train. Whoever had pushed him over was now standing above him in the line of fire of his troops. Quickly he regained his balance and aimed his pulse rifle, before lowering his weapon and breathing a sigh of relief. It was Bryan O'Neil, the arms dealer. The tension had soon left the entire squad as they too realised who it was. Bryan stumbled around before he tripped over his own two feet. His head was spinning and his eyes were sore from the overhead lights after being trapped inside the darkness. Baker reached down and pulled Bryan to his feet. Still disorientated he wobbled, unsure of where he was.

"Where am I?"

Baker chuckled at the confused man, feeling a slight pang of pity for the ordeal he must be going through.

"Well you just stumbled out of the docking bay and banged into me."

He noticed the dark patches around his eyes from where he had possibly been bound. The large red bump on his temple suggested he had been either struck on the head or had taken a bad fall. Bryan took a brief moment to regain his memory.

"It was those thugs!" he remembered, "Yes, I didn't sell them weaponry so they grabbed me and locked me in here before switching off the lights, those bastards!"

Baker stopped chuckling, realising just how serious the situation had become and questioned him further.

"Can you remember who it was? Any faces you recognise?" he asked eagerly.

Bryan stroked his pepper coloured beard and rubbed his head.

"No, but there were a lot of them…my store! I need to check on it urgently!" he gasped.

Baker put a reassuring hand on Bryan's shoulder,

"Not to worry old boy, we'll have them behind bars before you know it." His reassuring comment was broken by the clanging of metal deep within the darkened room of the docking bay. The tension swept back over the squad as their laser sights scanned the inside of the shadowy bay. Bryan hid behind Baker; his nerves were still not at their best. Baker moved inside the docking bay. The shadows felt suffocating. *Where the hell are the lights in this place?*

The clanging of metal was replaced with a loud hiss that sliced through Baker's thoughts. His squad were now at the doors, their stretched silhouettes under his feet. The painful silence continued as he crept further into the complex. His finger twitched on the trigger; if there were terrorists here he was going to do his damn best to send them to holy eternity. Reaching for the flash light located under his rifle he flicked the switch and light flooded the docking bay. He wasn't expecting what he was now witnessing. A cryo-tube sat like an ominous presence slanted at a low angle directly in front of where he was standing. It was completely empty.

"Sarge, I found the lights," a loud voice called as brightness swamped the area.

Slowly the flood lights activated, each one making their distinctive click and flooding further parts of the docking bay. As each one turned on, more and more cryo-tubes were revealed. They stretched the full length of the docking bay, all of them identical. The surrounding troops stared in awe as the full cargo of cryo-tubes was uncovered from the shadows. Neon blue digital numbers were placed on the upper sections of the blocky cylinders. Baker glanced at numbers 1 to 4 before being brought to both an unexpected and excited halt. Number 5 had a light layer of frost obscuring the glass, hiding whatever lay inside. Baker approached the cryo-tube and wiped his hand across it.

A large helmet stared back as he cleared more of the reinforced glass pane. By now all the soldiers and even Bryan had gathered around the tube and waited to see what lay inside. As he continued his clearing, more of the contents became visible, revealing a large and stocky polished white robot of human form. On his chest was the laser engraved roman numeral of two. Searching lower he found a data card containing the information he had been searching for. It read:

CARGO SHIPMENT 5
HORIZON VESSEL STOCK
CONTENTS: MPCD   CODENAME: TANK MARK 2
PROPERTY OF THE ALPHA TEAM SECTION
CAUTION – HEAVY PACKAGE, HANDLE WITH CARE

Baker looked up meaningfully at his squad and at Bryan before quickly checking all the remaining cryo-tubes, soon discovering that they were all empty. *Except this one.*

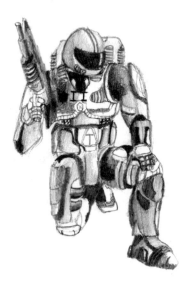

• Tank Mark 2 •

"This doesn't make any sense; first terrorists and now this. Did they bring it here?"

Looking around Baker found only puzzled expressions and so he decided that Charles best know about this. He radioed in by tapping the comm. on his helmet.

"Charles, this is Sergeant Baker of the HAF military, would you mind explaining to me just what the reason is for transporting an MPCD onboard a human travel cruiser?"

Charles replied almost instantaneously,

"There is no record in the Horizon database for any cargo concerning military weapons or machines, or the MPCD you have mentioned."

There was a moment of silence before Charles added,

"Someone else brought it here…"

At that moment the interior of the cryo-tube began to glow; inside Tank was starting to waken.

"I am Tank Mark 2." His robotic voice boomed through the large cryo-tube in which he was enveloped…

Chapter IX
A New World

John signalled to Catriona through the dim lighting, and she squirmed forwards on all fours towards the hatch. Now was their chance – the terrorists had departed with the captives they had gathered from the Horizon, herding them like sheep to an unknown fate. With the camp empty, their only chance was *now*.

"See – the path is clear. If we're going to try anything, there's no time like the present."

Catriona perched beside the hatch, her bright golden eyes scanning the outside air. She looked like a bird of prey under the morning light as it shone upon her.

"I'm all for your crazy ideas, as long as they get us out of here." She edged further towards him. "There has to be a way. That's what my father always told me – I've finally found a time to put his advice to good use." She fingered her dark tunic.

"We've got to break these wires," John instructed as he tested the bonds by extending his arms. They held firm and refused to loosen.

He examined the enclosure – a small supply room with poor lighting and few items left untouched. Catriona managed to tuck herself up into a tight bundle, and was momentarily lost in a twist of limbs.

"What are you doing?" John watched in awe as she unfolded herself with such expertise that he couldn't help wondering why she hadn't attempted it before.

"Didn't know I had it in me," she answered. She had

managed to get her restricted arms in front of her, while John still flailed with great effort, but his wrists knotted at his back. With a little guidance, he was able to perform just as successfully, and they found themselves facing the storage room door, with a mixture of caution and excitement.

"I would love to see the looks on their faces if they came back and found that we had escaped," Catriona said while they worked in unison, untying the binding wires that clamped them up. John wrenched the door open and climbed forward through the silent interior of the ship. He momentarily schemed to drive the Dark Sun transport vehicle, but the disadvantages of doing so tipped against them– they could easily be tracked, and neither had any idea how to pilot it – too risky.

They rushed outside into the morning light, breathing the alien air; it seemed to nourish them, and strange organisms drifted carelessly all around. Moving into the wilderness, they encountered a series of sights that were incomparable to anything they had ever witnessed before – the forestation and wildlife on Pharsee was amazing. Even Catriona, who no doubt had been acquainted with nothing other than the most beautiful of sights being the Captain's daughter, was breathless – a land of nature ungoverned by human science, necessities and comforts. A wonderful place.

John found the beckoning of the wild irresistible. Deep into the outer fringes of the forest, they found themselves in areas where foliage had sprouted to several times their size. Eternally grateful to be out of the reach of those that had killed so many, John and Catriona lay spread across an open grassy plain after a long trek from the terrorist camp, on the outskirts of the huge growths that lay ahead. John had tried to get across the importance of distance many times to her, but Catriona lay oblivious to the dangers behind and how fast they could catch up with them. In a second, danger showed its baleful face again.

Screaming overhead, a crimson shuttle of obvious alien origin broke the air as it flew at speeds great enough to push aside the plants beneath it. A small orb attachment, mounted on its rear, scanned the plains below, of its own accord. John grasped Catriona's arm and kicked off across the open plains, desperately seeking the cover of the forest so they could remain hidden.

A huge blue arc of light spouted out of the end of the shuttle as it closed in on them. John leapt ahead to avoid it, and could feel the intense heat on his calves as it cratered the plain a few feet behind him. Catriona screamed, alarming him of a second shot from the aircraft. It would have been a direct hit if they hadn't reached the high trees – many of which collapsed like matches under the unprovoked assault.

They hid in a large alcove under a huge twisting plant, where Catriona once again made the assumption that they were safe.

"I think we've lost them." She ran her fingers over her scalded cheek – it had blistered when a round of energy had passed close above her, striking the trees further ahead.

There was a clicking noise from above, but they ignored it and moved purposefully deeper into the woods. She shook her head fretfully.

"That was close – what was that thing?" John looked at her as if she knew all the answers.

"You think this has something to do with me?" She gaped unbelievingly.

"I just thought maybe you would have an idea of what it is if you had seen something like it before. We should have kept moving." She averted her eyes from him.

"I don't know who you are." It seemed a cruel remark to him – and something that hurt him deeply. Before he could respond, several small glinting objects struck her breasts, and she dropped without hesitation.

"Catriona!" he kneeled beside her, scanning the trees around him in search of the attackers. There was not a stir in the woods – and he knew it was unlikely that he would be able to protect them both, but he had to try, for her sake at least.

Slinging her over his shoulder and finding her surprisingly burdensome, he strode hurriedly in the opposite direction from where she had been struck. His heart raced and he felt feverish as their assailants allowed him to tread restlessly into the humid depths where plants grew to monstrous sizes. When he began to assume that he had avoided whoever had attacked them, he saw three deadly silver shapes on course for him. Before he could move, he was struck repeatedly and fell beside Catriona, deep among the huge alien foliage.

Chapter X
Enter, the Alpha Team

While repairs were underway on the battle damaged Horizon, Charles zipped through the air with very little time to spare. He was heading towards a medical bay to check up on the Captain. When he arrived, the Captain was already out of his bed and dressed in his uniform, ready for duty.

"Captain, with all due respect, you can barely look after yourself, never mind the Horizon, leave it to me. You've only been in the bay for five hours, forty three minutes and sixteen seconds, and some of the wounds you received when the terrorists attacked need more attention, although I can gladly confirm that none of them are life-threatening," Charles stated.

"Spare me the details Charles, those terrorist bastards have my daughter and I'll do whatever it takes to get her back. That includes running this ship."

The Captain paused and took a sip of the coffee he had picked up on his way out of the medical quarters. It filtered slowly down his throat and warmed the insides of his stomach; he closed his eyes and indulged in its comfort. 'KSK' was the name of the coffee – (Kick Start Koffee) because it boasted a developed stimulant mixture that awakened even the most weary ship commander. He could remember the famous advert that went – *KSK, the coffee with a 'k' that'll kick start your day.* The Captain shook his head. *Adverts these days, anything for publicity,* he thought and continued his conversation with Charles.

"Charles, what's the report on the Horizon?" he asked.

"The Horizon has suffered greatly and most of her docking bays are out of order. Being time-efficient because of my programming I have managed to restore the command centre to working order. I have ordered every civilian to proceed to the emergency department for a routine safety drill. As for the guards and marines, we have warned them to be on high alert and all weaponry, excluding firearms under development, are to be ready for immediate use. The engineers are working round-the-clock and we have had an encouraging response from on-board personnel in an effort to repair the damaged decks. I would also like to inform you that we suffered considerable casualties and that John has not been sighted since he was taken hostage – from this I can only deduce that he was kidnapped by the terrorists along with your daughter. Our scanners indicate two personnel alive on the planet Pharsee who are currently in sector five, on the outskirts of the Java Islands."

The Captain paused, tilted his head and sighed.

"Charles you don't know how relieved I am to hear that, thank you. I don't know what I would do without you. I want an immediate rescue team sent down to the planet!" he demanded.

"I've already sent for the team, sir. On this topic, do you know something peculiar came up today? I bet you weren't aware that there was an MPCD aboard this ship."

"I heard about some unexpected cargo being brought onboard by the Marvel but I didn't hear anything about this. What make is it?"

"He," Charles corrected. "He is the only second generation model, the most advanced combat machine to date," Charles added, once again displaying his knowledge in a blatantly obvious manner.

Perhaps I'll screw with his mainframe a little, the Captain thought smugly.

"Captain?"

"Yes?"

"You seem to be amused by something?"

"Ehh, no… where were we?" he muttered.

"Your lack of sleep has obviously become a drawback," Charles speculated.

"Hmmm, yes, quite, but it does help me conjure up some interesting ideas."

"Such as?"

"Oh, nothing. *He,* did you say?" The Captain asked with a most puzzled look on his face.

"That's right, he - the recent improvements in robotic technology have lead to his creation – a one-of-a-kind 'experiment', if you like. There simply wasn't sufficient time to continue production of this specific model before the Cion raided earth."

"Is he up and running then?" the Captain asked

"Yes."

"Where is he?"

"He has just left docking bay 9 accompanying Bryan O'Neil, the arms dealer who set up in business onboard the Horizon," Charles informed him.

For a brief moment the Captain remembered his encounter with Bryan. He remembered Bryan's reason for coming onboard the Horizon – he had jumped at the opportunity when a small network of shops had been established onboard. Bryan's previous business had involved state-of-the-art weapons and was going strong. But the business flourished when he moved onto the cruiser. The military onboard were Bryan's only real customers but there were also a few collectors here and there…

The Captain pulled himself together and was determined to find out what he was dealing with- how could he lead the people of the Horizon if he, too, did not know what was happening?

"Well, let's get back to the command centre. I want to meet this MPCD and find out how he got onboard, not to mention just what exactly he is doing here."

The Captain and Charles hastily left the medical bay and headed straight for the bridge…

On arrival the Captain moved towards his desk and sat himself down. Around him were the noticeable scars on the floor and desks from the fire-fight that taken place earlier and which resulted in the kidnapping of both John and his daughter. He let out a remorseful sigh.

Will Robinson, the radar operator noticed George's grief,

"Sir, no matter how bad things turned out back there, it wasn't your fault. You are a Captain unlike any other, and you have many responsibilities. I know I can't begin to understand what you're going through right now, but I urge you not to be demoralised by this. The people still look up to you - remember that." Robinson nodded, turned around and continued his scan of the area surrounding the Horizon. George would see that all those that had helped after the terrorist incursion were rewarded for their services.

The Captain felt comforted by this remark and, with a new confidence, sat up and began a check-up analysis of the Horizon's structural damage. His mind, however, was still on other things. He asked himself questions, like would he ever see his daughter, or was she hurt or worse- dead, and for what twisted purpose did she and John serve in the scheme of things? The Captain was going through hell – it was just one disaster after another since John had arrived. The voyage had gone smoothly up to that point, and he was in line for a very generous pay-packet. He still hadn't gotten over the arrival of that man, and John was still to be told of what the recent test-updates Charles had received this morning displayed.

Suddenly the air-lift access panel began to glow. Apprehensively, the Captain watched as two figures dropped onto the command deck.

On the left the Captain immediately recognised Bryan O'Neil- he looked rough and shaken, but he was a tough guy and a survivor.

On the right- a white armoured giant measuring over two metres tall marched alongside him, down the small pathway towards the Captain's desk. The Captain, seeing this machine for the first time, was impressed by the robot's sheer bulk, yet felt intimidated by his towering appearance.

The two new arrivals continued up the pathway, unaware that they had most of the command crew's attention upon entering. They reached the Captain's desk and halted.

George reached out and shook hands with the pair of them and requested that they sit down. Bryan couldn't refuse and slumped himself in the seat, rustling his rear, trying to make himself comfortable. The robot remained standing.

The Captain offered Bryan a drink of KSK... he sure needed it. Gratefully accepting the aromatic drink, he took several gulps and allowed the stuff to do its thing. He watched as the Captain began to question Tank.

"Robot, identify yourself."

The machine stood perfectly still, his helmet covering his facial expressions. The machine's robotic voice reverberated through the command centre,

"MPCD- classification-Tank Mark 2."

The Captain pondered on the name for a moment - the famous Tank model. If he was remembering correctly the Mark 1 had been used in the Cion conflict, but since then no information regarding the machine was ever recorded. The only known fact was that it had bought time for the ships to escape from Cion control. Presumed either destroyed or captured, the machine had been lost in combat. After that time it had only been mentioned in robotics and history classes, proving that not all machines would turn on their human creators. The Mark 1 had shown that through self-sacrifice.

However, more questions needed answers.

"How did you get onboard? And who authorised it?"

Tank responded automatically.

"I was placed onboard the Marvel by the Section of Defence after we departed from Earth in order to escape the Cion assault swarms. I was recently transported to this cruiser and designated to docking bay 9, a blind spot to the ships sensors."

The Captain stroked the stubble on his chin realising that this had to be part of a very well thought out plan. His questions continued,

"But why all the secrecy?"

"There was a danger of running into the Cion again and a risk of capture, so I was placed on the Marvel as it had an eighty percent chance of escape, the highest of the five cruisers departing from the failing planetary defences. If my presence was known to the people of the ship, it might have caused conflict on safety grounds. The Cion could have picked up any signals coming from the transmitter that broadcasts news on the Marvel, and my existence onboard the ship could have been revealed to all eyes. Might I add sir, that we were still on Earth which was falling under Cion control before we escaped and made the jump to Logar. After docking at Logar the military sent an undercover team falsely presented as a group of engineers to withdraw me from the cruiser while it was being revamped. I was regarded as priority one cargo that needed a cover up story to avoid any major incidents such as theft, destruction, accidental damage or loss. A twenty year process was sufficient time to further advance my abilities and develop new technology within the base of Logar. Once development protocol classified 'Human Shield' had neared its completion stages I was placed into the hands of a rescue team who had purchased me for their own uses. Their reasons for placing me onboard this cruiser afterwards are questions I do not yet possess the answers for," Tank carefully explained.

The Captain still had memories of that fateful day - E-Day (Evacuation Day) when five human galactic cruisers, 'Horizon', 'Distance', 'Star Lance', 'Flare' and 'Marvel' made a desperate attempt to escape Earth by flying through the Cion Assault Grid and making a light-speed jump to Logar. The images of 'Star Lance' as it slowly crumbled and withered under the incoming assault, its eventual detonation which killed the countless people onboard, still burned fresh in the Captain's mind. 'Star Lance's' destruction was not in vain, as the four remaining cruisers escaped intact to Logar. Logar was a new planet occupied by humans which still remained a secret from the Cion forces, and hopefully would stay that way.

Once again the Captain found himself thinking about his daughter …

"Ship approaching docking bay 6, classification – Alpha one Permission to dock?" a voice came from around the area; it was the computer requesting clearance for the vessel to approach.

"Permission granted," George said.

After questioning Tank, he averted his attention to Bryan, who by the looks of things was more or less back to his usual self. Bryan set the cup on the table, half-full; the Captain could still smell the familiar scent of KSK.

"What happened at the docking bay, Bryan? Charles briefly

went over the incident with me and apparently you were found locked in docking bay 9."

Bryan sat up and locked eyes with the Captain.

"Well Captain, sir, I was on my way back to the weapons depot for my second shift of work when I ..." Bryan paused in mid-sentence, his mind still confused about those events.

"Bryan?" the Captain asked in an attempt to bring him back to his senses.

Startled, Bryan recollected the events and then answered,

"Thugs, vandals, bastards, whatever you call them!"

The Captain closed his eyes, lowered and shook his head.

"Yes, it seems there is always a thorn amongst the roses, and this thug problem is getting out of hand."

"Damnit, I still haven't been able to return to my store. Not that there will be much left to see anyway, once those buggers get a hold of everything," he muttered.

Charles beeped twice.

"The team are here, shall I send for them?" he interrupted.

"Yes, of course, call them up," George answered.

The white light of the air-lift was glowing once more and four figures slowly emerged. Three men and a machine moved forwards until they were within talking distance of the Captain.

"Captain, Alpha team reporting for duty sir. Glad to see you're still in one piece Tank," the white armoured man said to the towering robot.

"Like-wise," Tank replied.

Tank approached the team, turned around and faced the Captain, who watched keenly as the Alpha team pulled together– Calron was the white armoured figure, his face concealed by a white-metal helmet with a cyan shaped 'T' glowing defiantly in the middle. He had a large pistol clipped to his belt, some of the strangest gauntlets the Captain had ever seen, a dagger positioned on the side of his boot and some sort of shield implemented into a sword on his back. He bore the mark of the team on his chest and shoulder armour – a sharp, metallic, yet simply designed, 'A' that had few distinguishable qualities. To his right was yet another bizarrely dressed human-he wore a cloak, an armoured plated suit and a mask which covered his mouth and nose. He carried an ornate staff. He was known as Adaman- the manner in which he was presented made him look like something from mythology. He, too, bore a bladed weapon on his back; an extravagant katana inlaid with precious stones. The Captain could just see the end of the blade peering out behind the stranger's robes. The third was easily recognised as a military combatant, embellished in dark brown armour, holding an assault rifle similar to that of the guards' weaponry. The soldier seemed at ease, yet the additional scoped rifle on his back reinforced the Captain's overall first impression- this guy meant serious business; you don't carry weapons of such a dangerous variety around with you merely for display purposes. His dark brown helmet had a reflective visor on the front and a re-breather which only humans wore – this man had been named Trooper Brown – he was the last of the Delta left after the failed assassination attempts on the Cion commander. The rest of his previous team had been brutally slaughtered by the Cion upon discovery of their plans. He bore both the mental and physical scars of that event, yet Trooper Brown rarely spoke of it. He wore small remnants of his previous team's suits like a symbol of his sorrow, but deep down this had only made him stronger; it was a constant reminder of the vow he had made to avenge them. To his left was the robot- ninja like in form, his metal body was covered by purple and black metal plating with a bizarre dark symbol engraved on his chest. The robot was staring directly at the Captain, his face nothing but a visor. A hollow aura seemed present in the air around this robot, as if it harboured some terrible dark secret. The Captain knew he had nothing to be scared of but felt uncomfortable under the thing's glare – he was face to face with the machine which had known many a conquest. Because of its exceptional combat skills, it had been given the name Slayer.

• Slayer •

Not exactly what the Captain was expecting for a rescue team, but he reassured himself by recalling the stories he had heard involving this group and, by all accounts, they were the best in the business. As the saying goes-'Don't judge a book by its cover.'

Chapter XI
Cursed Blessings

Deep within the confines of the Gatheren flagship, the supreme lord Arbus Wrathen stood gazing fixatedly out of one of the many heavily armoured viewing ports, directly at Pharsee. He was the highest ranking member of the Gatheren. However, such a position did not come without sacrifice and Arbus had suffered greatly for it.

He had lost his mortality. Now he had become an embodiment of energies that had been the result of a freak occurrence during the time of the Ocorius Conflict.

This was due to one of the Gatheren modes of travel - portal. This hazardous method of jumping from planet to planet through gaps in time was about to alter Arbus forever.

During the cleansing of the comet Ocorius, a lone Reptan soldier had survived the merciless ambush of the Mites. He would be forever known as Arbus Wrathen, the undeniable ruler of the Gatheren from that day forth. On a quest to return to his home planet Gathera, he had attempted to jump through the portal during a severe storm. As his body materialised he had escaped from Ocorius and was able to return home to tell the civilisation of the fate of his fellow kin. As he neared complete materialisation the storm had become attracted to the portal dome. The quarter sphere drew in the energy of a lighting strike and had focused this on Arbus' body. The event stripped him of all emotions and flesh, tearing mortality away from him and leaving him as a wandering spirit. As he travelled through time the rock that had been blasted with him was forged to become the basis of his body. His weapons had become augmented by the violent storm; the sheer power of nature had become part of his essence, his very being.

He was Reptan no more.

As he was robbed of the parts that made him alive he was re-assembled at the opening of the portal dome in Gathera. The spectacle was hailed as a momentous occasion by the Gatheren who waited for the return of the attack squad A*5. They now believed a God had been called to lead them to victory and they saw this being as one of great strength, wisdom and utterly fearless. Arbus could not come to terms with what had happened to him and in a fit of insanity roared with rage and tensed a new body. The Gatheren merely celebrated his apparent show of eminence. They did not understand that in actual fact he was calling for help, begging for some way of escape from this new 'iron body'. He had become massive, easily over three metres tall, and was covered in black and grey forged metal in which his spiritual flames were encased for all eternity.

Confusion had become deeply rooted inside his mind, as he had altered completely; no longer did he breathe air, no longer could he feel the ground beneath his feet. Collapsing to the floor, the celebrations died. Flames dripped from his body, the ground beneath him cracked and shook; the surrounding crowds of mixed species reeled in a mixture of fear and awe. Believing the only comrades who understood him had died on Ocorius, he grasped the dusty ground beneath him, clenching it so tight it was set alight within his palm before becoming ash that whispered between his large fingers. He couldn't feel it; the flames were nothing, no burns or scabs appearing…no pain, no sense of touch – nothing!

What have I become? He questioned himself, absolutely dumbstruck by this supposed miracle that the surrounding crowds insisted on calling it. *Miracle!? This is no miracle, this is a CURSE! I'm cursed and you do nothing!*

Throwing himself back to his feet he noticed the showers of eyes were still staring at him, waiting expectantly for some sort of acknowledgement. Instead Arbus reached his arms out to discover yet another truly terrifying aspect of his new body; his right arm had become the most ornate weapon he had laid his single eye upon. Weightless, perfectly carved, it struck him to find a single symbol seemed to dominate the back. Reaching for his face he discovered it, too, had changed – three horns protruded from the sides and rear of his alien skull. No longer able to contain any more unanswered questions within, Arbus begun to stride forward, his mighty feet creating thundering claps as he moved through the crowd that gave way before him. Approaching the nearest building, its sheen momentarily obscured his reflection but cleared away as he looked at it from a different angle. Gazing at the reflection an alien entity stared back – he now saw clearly what he had become.

• Arbus •

He is a God ... a spectacle ... a warrior ... magnificent ... welcomed! Voices chanted inside his mind. He turned back to the growing crowd; none spoke but he could mentally hear their voices. They were pawns; he could have easily decimated the entire crowd. Anger pumped through his newly assembled body.

No, it's not them, the Clam – the tool of deceit! It did this, my brothers, my family, it lied!

Arbus did not stop for anyone or anything; heading for the Tower of Eyes- one of the most sacred structures on Gathera, he picked up pace. Now he was leaping over buildings and crowds alike. Fear and confusion spread through the population like a terrible plague, and they knew from the way he had stared at the towering structure *exactly* where he had planned on going. Obeying orders from the leaders, ground troops tracked down this new threat, believing their weapons and abilities were sufficient enough to stall him. But Arbus was outrunning any on-foot infantry unit that tried to prevent him from completing his mission – to destroy the Clam. The familiar noise of soaring howlers sliced overhead; the sleek aircraft had large claw like objects situated on their top rear halves. Crimson in colour, giving the aircraft an intimidating and menacing appearance, their 'blessed weapons' were believed to not only reduce victims to ash but to rip the souls from their bodies as they were burnt alive. Rotating their deadly weapons quickly, their target was clear and thus they emitted powerful streaks of laser fire directly at it. Dodging the incoming streams of heat, buildings were scorched, tankers erupted and detonated as the misplaced shots went wide of their target. Throughout the smoke and fire that rose metres high, Arbus crouched, biding his time, hidden from their watchful gaze.

The noise overhead grew as the howlers flew in for a second strike. Waiting for the precise moment, Arbus found that he could see the aircraft as clear as day through the smoke, yet another ability he had only now just uncovered. When the ships were almost directly above him he sprung from the charred ground and emerged from the black smoke billowing in the air. Not realising the danger, the aircraft continued their patrol in the standard 'W' formation. The front vessel shot abruptly upwards as a massive flame blasted its way through the hull, incinerating the pilot. Ablaze and torn apart, the remains of the howler plummeted towards the buildings below. The formation broke apart as the ship's Reptan pilots realised the fire demon's intent. Dividing up, the pilots sacrificed combined firepower for survival, an effective tactic to stay unpredictable against their opponents. Arbus knew this well and that it would be their downfall. Landing swiftly and with the grace of a falcon, he slipped between the spherical buildings, still heading towards the tower. One armed officer, Magnel Regbel, ordered his fellow wingmen to engage the creature…by any means necessary in order to protect the Tower of Eyes. Turning his ship on the spot, the strangest idea occurred to him. Unpredictability was a successful tactic to use in the air but this was a ground based target. He glanced at his severed left arm – the vile filth that was the Mites did this, slicing off the lower half of his forearm and then ripping it apart in front of him, before swallowing it crudely. Honour and pride swelled inside his body, accompanied by sheer hatred for the creatures, gripping him into a frenzy of madness and causing him to continue his assault on the monstrosity. He tore the Mite with such ease it gave him tremendous satisfaction to feel its cold blood run between his toes. Finding himself seated back in the cockpit of his howler, he regrouped his memories and buried them deep in his mind. Speaking to his fellow pilot who operated the claw weaponry, he informed his comrade in alien tongue.

"Gathera rack die! Come comrade!"

There was a moment of silence as the co-pilot received the request,

"With you!" she cackled madly.

The shuttle spun swiftly, searing the air as it raced towards the fire god who continued in his path. Magnel could have sworn he heard the sky wail as he applied full thrust to the aircraft. He dived in and out of gaps between buildings chasing his target – he would sooner have his life taken than miss it again. Arbus' consciousness warned him, causing him to turn and witness the speeding ship heading straight for him. He was startled to find who it was as the pilots leapt out of the aircraft on their suicide mission. The ship was still on course for Arbus as it careered on along the ground, sending small metal shards and sparks everywhere. The engines burst into flames and the already fast-advancing wreckage was thrown on an even more frantic collision course. Arbus looked on at the deadly but beautiful piece of warfare heading towards him. But then he felt his body speak to him, and slowly but purposefully it guided his movements with alien precision, as his ornate weapon glided across the hull of the vehicle, splitting it in two. The sensation was indescribable; it traversed from the pit of his spine until it gently caressed his mind. It was as if he had witnessed the act before it occurred, similar to human déjà vu. The halves swirled and continued to slide across the ground until they came to a sudden halt next to a travel tower. Through the flames came the two Reptans, ready to die in combat if need be now that they had performed the ritual. One of the Reptans had his honour blade as his left arm. At that moment Arbus discovered the identity of the warriors and lowered his weapon. With his guard down the female Reptan leapt towards him, taking advantage of the opportunity, but was cast aside when his colossal fist met her chest. Urel flopped and rolled, unconscious by the blow, before she eventually stopped next to the flaming wreckage. The sudden and frightening sound of a collapsing structure alerted them as the travel tower began to topple. The building's foothold had been significantly damaged from the collision and now it could no longer support itself. Magnel abandoned the conflict with the creature and headed to Urel in a desperate attempt to rescue her. The looming shadow stretched as the building neared collapse – it seemed determined to take the Reptans with it to an early grave. Hoisting her over his shoulder, Magnel stared at the ever-enlarging tower as it thundered its way downwards. He shut his eye and readied himself for death; there was no chance of escape… he waited… a loud crumbling suggested it was only a couple of seconds away. But death never came.

The searing heat of the fire licked at his exposed flesh as he opened his eye and turned to seize the chance he had been given. That was when he saw the being for who he truly was. Arbus towered over him, holding the collapsing building with his left arm. Magnel felt him speak in his mind.

Magnel Regbel, it is I, Arbus. Hurry!

Not waiting to understand this demon, he made haste away from the hazardous zone and into safety, still clutching Urel. The violent crash of the building echoed behind and he turned to see Arbus striding off into the distance, still heading for the Tower of Eyes. Clicking on his distance comm. he alerted the fellow Reptan pilots to break off chase and return home. As he lifted Urel up he found himself disbelieving what he had just seen.

What has become of him? Magnel thought in horror, unable to find any answers.

● ● ●

Now at the bottom of the Tower of Eyes, the weather took a turn for the worse. Overhead the sky became submerged in heavy grey clouds and the rain poured down on cue. Lightning struck at the far corners of the world, and dancing forks flickered and wavered for split second intervals. The icy winds scraped by, working its way into nooks and crannies between the many buildings that littered the area. Arbus paid it no heed as he carefully looked over the entrances, considering the different ways in which he could breach its hidden defences. Leaping up to the second floor helped him get a better view of the inside, as he peered through the windows, taking into account just how many guards there were. Large Tyrans lay asleep on the ground, their Reptan masters marching on patrol, ready to awaken the slumbering beasts in order to protect the leaders and the Great Clam from intruders. Arbus could have just fought his way upwards to reach the Chamber of the Lords and then dictate from there; they were expecting him to do just that but as he was preoccupied with the guards below, the lords would have time to unleash the power of the Clam on Arbus, rendering him useless. He could tell this from their over-confident thoughts. No, this time required him to stay hidden in the shadows. His inner flames died, blending his dark body in with the stormy weather. Hesitating no longer, he realised that the only way up was to climb on the outer wall. As he started to climb his body once again spoke to him requesting that he place his hand on the metallic wall that stretched above him. His hand moved effortlessly and attached to the wall like a magnet drawn to the small particles of energy surrounding the structure. Looking upwards he could see the spectacular crystals that lay high atop the building – they shone like diamonds, providing light that illuminated his face. They glittered like the eyes of a colossal being, hence the name the Tower of Eyes. Arbus stopped. Why did something so blatantly obvious not occur to him? He stared at his right arm - how would he pull himself up against the wall if he had no right arm to do so? As if his arm had heard his question it shook uncontrollably and set itself alight with flames so stubborn the rain itself sizzled away as the droplets of water failed to suffocate them. His beautiful weapon submerged itself into his body, sinking inwards to reveal his right arm. The flames died. Clenching his fist, he glanced upwards to the crystals and started once again to climb. He never looked back.

Inside, the leaders of the Gatheren were seated in large oval chairs. They were from all the different species that had united to form the collective race. Each represented the colonies that played a vital part in the on-going wars that raged across the galaxy, the most terrible being the Great Mite Wars. As the storms raged outside, the leaders were all seated comfortably in the tranquillity of the Great Clam. It was a display of the purest of colours, dazzling to behold, yet also resplendent. The large Clam possessed such knowledge that it had been able to manipulate the leaders of the colonies in order to obtain such high status. It accurately provided information on planets and their dwellers - this in turn had given the Gatheren the perfect map, allowing them to direct assaults on their sworn enemies with ruthless efficiency. However, the Clam had now changed its own overall strategy. Now it requested that the Gatheren take out small Mite locations that had only formed it the last few years. Little did the Gatheren know that it had picked the first and most dominant of the Mite habitats –one thousand year old comets that travelled the length of the universe housing countless numbers of the intolerable and hostile creatures. It was slowly killing the Gatheren race in order to achieve its own mysterious and unfathomable goals. But little did it know that one warrior had survived and knew the truth.

And that he was now outside the window where it took residence…

The patter of the raindrops bounced unnoticed off Arbus'

shoulders, trickling down the length of his body. He stared directly at the Clam, unable to control his hatred. His sword emerged from his body and with it he smashed through the large window and crashed into the chamber, surprising all inside. A moment's silence was disturbed by a lightning strike just outside, bringing everyone back to their senses. Guards hastily made their way upwards towards the chamber. Knowing this, Arbus was instinctively led by his body towards the doors. Swinging his fist, the doors bent outwards and jammed, preventing both outside help from arriving and any leader escaping. The thudding of the guards outside as they feverishly tried to gain entrance played on in the background. One of the leaders found the courage to stand up and face the supposed threat that had just entered. The Reptan leader Knarlock was dressed in ornamental gold plating, accompanied by ruby red robes and a black cape. He stood to face Arbus who towered over him, staring directly at him as if he took insult from such an act.

"In the name of all that is the Gatheren, identify yourself!" he ordered whilst simultaneously activating his honour blade. His tone was deep; signifying the great age and respect he had come to be associated with. Arbus was impressed by his courage; he was indeed suited to lead the Reptan colony. But that did not affect the matter. He had become blinded by the Clam and needed to hear the truth. Arbus strode over towards the so called 'Great Clam'. Its silver pearl colour made it look a thing of beauty but Arbus knew better.

"You are all blinded by this manipulative creature; it serves us no greater purpose than the Mites themselves. I will make you see!" Arbus brought up his sword and plunged downwards on the Great Clam that, in the heat of the moment, revealed its true colours.

The shell became a ghastly purple, and tentacles sprouted

from all parts of its body. They bound around Arbus, wrestling him to the ground as it peeled itself away from the tiled floor. The once resting Clam had now become a thing of monstrous evil. It pinned Arbus to the ground, holding him in place as it brought out yet another horrific part of its body. The pearl had mutated into an edged weapon that glowed at irregular intervals. Around, the leaders had backed towards the far corners of the chamber staying away from the conflict unfolding before them. Arbus' body shook, his mighty flames showering his torso, escaping out through any available gaps in his armour. He too glowed, but it was brighter and more stunning than the Clam had ever been. Dark silhouettes were cast on the walls as the duo wrestled on the ground, cracking the tiles and ornamental plates that lay in their path. In a quick but purposeful movement, Arbus catapulted the mutated Clam through the leaders' chairs and out of the opposite window through which he had come in. Rising from the ground, he noticed the Clam clambering back in. By now the guards had smashed their way through and the lumbering Tyrans were directed inwards. Arbus leapt through the chamber, his loin cloth trailing behind and slammed into the Clam yet again. The pair wrestled and fought with a vicious quality never seen before, and the guards were left not knowing who to attack. The balcony crumbled as blows were missed and slashes dodged. Seeing an attack Arbus ducked, avoiding the tentacle that crashed into the wall removing sizable chunks that littered the already battle-scarred balcony. Now open, Arbus upper cut the creature directly in the torso, sending it reeling into the wall of the balcony. Dust and rubble dropped downwards onto the gathering crowds that had piled around the Tower of Eyes. They spread out like a group of scattered marbles, fleeing the debris. A tentacle wrapped around Arbus' sword arm and dragged him off the balcony. The two rolled and slammed off the wall, splitting statues of heroes and smashing windows as they tumbled downwards, dropping like lead weights. They still fought furiously as they clutched one another. The crowds moved further away as the duo thundered their way downwards before colliding with the ground below. Debris was now split into smaller chunks and dust filled the air, obscuring the battle. A painful silence took hold except for the chattering of rubble as it landed on top of the battle scene. Rain still lashed down, splattering the crowds below. The dust never seemed to clear until a large figure, easily recognisable, marched on through, dragging the wriggling remnants of his enemy behind. The fire god stopped to face the crowds,

"I am Arbus Wrathen and I have freed you…" he dropped the corpse of the defeated Clam. "Now is the dawning of a new era that shall see us smite our greatest foes. Any opposition shall be crushed!"

Roars and cheers unexpectedly burst out. He looked at his people. With this declaration Arbus had now created a new empire – his empire! The title of supreme lord was granted to him at a ceremony the following day. The once stubborn Knarlock now looked upon this new leader with great expectation. The title was sealed as he spread a fresh new cape across Arbus' shoulders. It slowly dropped downwards into place, dangling just above the ground. *Perfect match.*

"We have been blessed to have received you. I apologise on my behalf for ever doubting you," he muttered quietly, just loud enough for Arbus to hear. Arbus acknowledged this and placed a large but appreciative hand gently on the Reptan leader's shoulder. The ceremony was brought to a close. His sword – the Withering Hollows - was carved into the newly assembled section of the Tower of Eyes, believed to aid his leadership as well as display it.

He noticed the symbol that dominated the back of his weapon once again…

Chapter XII
Buried Secrets

The Horizon's hull and interior was still having maintenance work done on it. It drifted above planet Pharsee like a lost soul. Inside the Captain briefed the team on their objectives and informed them of an alien race that the Human Alliance Forces met nearly a hundred years ago- similar to humans, this race was called Bigadons. Years ago Bigadons told of a conflict that was responsible for wiping out not only their populace established on the planet Seeth, but the humans living there as well. They described it as if the stars had just become enraged, plummeting towards the planet and destroying everything. Historians were still, to this day, trying desperately to piece together the few remnants left of the puzzle concerning that event and the 'evil people' the Bigadons referred to. What they had found out was that the stars didn't drop; it was the actions of a hostile alien race intent on destruction – a race known as the Gatheren.

Trooper Brown's impatience was palpable - his body language made this clear. Nevertheless this was one of his more admirable qualities, always being eager to start the mission and rescue lives. Seeing this the Captain continued,

"We've also had an amazing stroke of luck amidst everything else that's been happening here, believe it or not. Bigadons have already colonised this planet, establishing themselves in this section here," the Captain took a moment to pause and brought up a holographic global map of the planet. Carefully he typed in the code and the team watched attentively as the screen flickered, before displaying a shower of data. The wealth of information now present showed the landscape of the planet; the most obvious part being the highlighted area surrounded by a red circle. The screen then focused on this point and enlarged the selected area. Soon a structure came into view; it was of enormous size and was not of natural formation. The team could tell this for sure.

"So this is where we are heading, yes?" Calron asked as he pointed at the massive alien Plaza on the holographic map. His finger passed through it causing it to haze up. He withdrew his hand and placed it by his side, waiting expectantly for a 'yes'.

"No," the Captain replied, contradicting him. "That is where you will rendezvous," he continued.

The screen suddenly withdrew from this location as the Captain typed away, and then brought a new one into view- a temple.

"This is where you will head to," the Captain said monotonously.

"A temple? Sir, If I wanted to pray for my sorry ass I could think of no better place to go," Trooper Brown sarcastically replied, narrowly avoiding insubordination.

The screen focused towards this new area, blue shapes which highlighted steel or some other sort of unnatural material appearing on screen.

After witnessing this, Trooper Brown decided from now on he would keep his mouth shut, at least in briefing rooms.

"Temples don't make themselves you know," the Captain added, replying to Trooper Brown's original sarcastic comment.

"Here is where Horizon's sensors have discovered human heat signals." The Captain recalled his lecture on this mysterious man 'John' to the team – he could confide matters of extreme secrecy to them without concern. He took a brief moment to breathe.

"I can only deduce from these signals that two hostages, who we suspect to be John and Catriona, are being held there. They're alive!"

"What about that base in the temple? If that's where the two humans are now being held, then it could pose a significant threat towards the Horizon and the Bigadon Empire on the planet, our supposed 'allies'. It would not be wise to leave it functional," Slayer advised.

"That's for the Bigadon infiltrator to take care of. When you head down towards the surface she will accompany you to the temple. Military action has already been considered but this is no ordinary, run-of-the-mill mission and our main military forces have been sent down to the planet to establish a landing zone on the outskirts of the Plaza. We simply can't let them think we're holding back on them."

"Don't the Bigadons have their own military?" Calron asked, intrigued.

"Yes, and quite a sizable one, but it's not stationed on Pharsee I'm afraid. But because their population here is perhaps the largest they have on any known planet, I wouldn't be surprised if it arrived suddenly. The Bigadons have always been a bit of a dark horse. Moving back to the case of our military," he said, as if he had been rudely interrupted, "there is only so much we can do. But we know that this temple structure is not of human or Bigadon design from what our ally intelligence has told us. Those captives are both of great importance to the HAF as well as to myself, and if it means accompanying a fellow missionary then so be it."

"Sir, with all due respect, I think we should handle this. I don't want any distractions. She'll probably only hold us back," Trooper Brown protested.

"Sorry, no choice Brown, you've got two hostages to rescue and I don't want to fall out with the Bigadons. An alliance with them is not something to be taken lightly. I'm pretty sure they know more about the hostiles than us so let them play their part in this one. They've allowed us to continue our mission without interference. They, too, have their own reasons for reaching this temple, so let's not miss out on the opportunity to get together on some common ground."

Trooper Brown gave a reluctant grunt before coming to a quiet acceptance of these terms. Tank and Slayer remained silent but knew that Trooper Brown had a point. Tank held a pulse rifle and shunted the clip underneath the barrel while Slayer ran checks on his strange weaponry.

"There's a lot at stake here, I can see that clearly, but this is something both new and dangerous, something you've possibly never come across before. Take care for all our sakes…dismissed," the Captain announced.

With that, the Team headed down to Docking Bay 6 and boarded the *Alpha One*. They strapped themselves in and for a brief moment they all paused to look at the interior of the marvellous vessel that was the Horizon. Firing up its engines, the machine sped out of the bay before turning around and rocketing down to the planet, on a very important mission… they all knew the dangers involved but this came with the job. Rescuing people now took on a new, more dangerous front.

The Captain sat himself down, gazing at the holo-panel which showed planet Pharsee in all its glory. He bit his bottom lip, nervously sweating, wishing the team and everyone else good luck…they were sure as hell going to need it…

Chapter XIII
When Things Go Wrong

When the Terrorists returned to camp, moods were not at their best. Ridley had personally discovered that their two most important hostages had gone missing. He growled malevolently and forced aside many of his edgy soldiers.

"What *heretic* was on guard duty while I was away?" he shouted.

"Dozer was, boss, but we can't find him anywhere." *The wimp must have run from his own shadow.* Ridley would see to it that he would make the rest of the recruit's life needlessly difficult should he be found.

"Do you realise the consequences of their escape? Because of this, the Captain of the Horizon has no obligation to cease fire on our ships. He'll be looking for us relentlessly – he won't think twice about blowing us to smithereens if we've got nothing to act as a back-stop."

"We could rally another few passengers onboard, boss," a sombre bulk of man suggested.

"I think Captain George will see that as a bargain in exchange for our deaths – a few of his nameless citizens aren't likely to play heavily on his conscience."

His anger swelled up inside him like a starving animal. He felt like thrusting his sword, *Anaconda,* into the nearest man who dared breathe out of place.

"Because of Dozer, we could very well be dead within the hour." He ground his teeth together threateningly – what had the fool been thinking, abandoning his tribe and his duty to

Ridley, a man who had taken him into the business of Dark Sun with open arms? Traitorous vermin.

"A bounty weapon upgrade will be awarded to any man who brings him to me *alive*." His men began gathering small weapons frantically before dispatching ahead into the outer ring of the forest, in search of the amateur recruit. No doubt Dozer wouldn't survive a week alone on this planet. Ridley considered killing him now as a personal favour.

But first he would see to it that his tracks were covered – being discovered by the superior military sky fleets of the Horizon would spell doom for them all.

Several minutes later, a veteran who had been doing his service dutifully for Dark Sun for many a year approached him, a man Ridley recognised as Jacob. He had a ghastly expression.

"Boss," he quivered. "We've found Dozer." Ridley met his gaze.

"Well bring him to me, in one piece." The man's expression did not change.

"That might be a bit hard, boss."

"And why is that?" he frowned quizzically as he examined the dark metal plating of his forearms.

"Someone must have got to him before we did."

● ● ●

Ridley stood over the violent murder scene, examining the hacked corpse of Dozer under a now-bloody tree. His limbs had been severed, and all that remained was a charred skeleton which was only identified as that of the young recruit because of the intact metal tag that dangled around his neck. The man had obviously fallen prey to a species with weaponry beyond their comprehension, as the trunks of trees around him had been cut at precise angles through the use of targeted lasers. The naïve officer was struck by something that had torn his skin from his skeleton and turned his blood to ash. Ridley bit down on his lip, disturbing thoughts surrounding him. Was there some other force that was playing a part in thwarting his plans? He hoped, with a passion for human caring he had never found in himself before, that no man under his employment ever had to suffer the same fate. He revoked his insults on the vulnerable recruit. But how did he manage to get all the way out here? Was he dragged to his death?

Tearing his nametag from the heap of bones, he clenched it hard in his gauntlets and peered into the distance.

Chapter XIV
Into the Ruins

Hidden within the mazes of an ancient temple, the Gatheren were upturning every object they came across like a child searching for its lost toy. They were, however, looking for something that would be the key to their survival. Multiple squads had broken off from the main search group to quicken the pace of uncovering. They began to proceed through the now-ruined outpost where communication had been stalled because of a recent and unexpected enemy incursion – the Mites appeared to be the most probable suspect.

They were in the believed-to-be Fera Grounds, a race that had supposedly once occupied this planet over three thousand years ago…

Leader Stoke lead his squadron on approach to the rally point. So far, there had been no sightings of their cunning antagonists, but that was only to be expected.

Dun, a squat Toxican, a lesser ranked species among the Gatheren military, prowled anxiously behind, his large gleaming eyes scanning over the shadows.

The Temple they explored was certainly like nothing they had ever seen before – a massive crystal structure of great age, almost like a palace, had got the Gatheren very excited – perhaps the planet dwellers from millennia past were not so much a bizarre and eccentric idea as once thought. Reptan Stoke ran his hand across one of the many walls inlaid with hieroglyphs, carefully brushing away sand and dust that had lain dormant for thousands of years. It ran down his armoured hand and danced at his feet. He examined the clear section of the wall, attempting to understand what was trying to be told in the strange shapes of a forgotten civilisation. He couldn't. Turning towards an excited Dun, he shook his head. Dun's anxiety soon left him as he stared back towards his superior.

"Is their anything there your excellence?"

"No, there's nothing but another of those worded walls," Stoke replied, his disappointment clearly etched on his reptilian face. He, too, was excited about the prospect of finding whatever it was that lay hidden on this mysterious planet. Their leader, Arbus, had seemed adamant that it was here - *it had to be here.*

Footsteps echoed through the musty corridors with accompanying silhouettes. Another Gatheren squad approached that of Stoke's. It was Azul Bagel accompanied by Zulu's search squad. On arrival of their commander, Stoke brought his squad to attention and waited for new orders.

Azul subtly waved his hand issuing an 'at ease' order resulting in Stoke's squad breaking into quiet conversation amongst themselves and their new arrivals. Azul, Zulu and Stoke began informing one another of how the operation was progressing in the search for their objective. Azul withdrew a sphere-glass and the trio devoted their attention to the mapped image of the temple inside.

"Our C*1 squadron has performed a sweeping search of this area," Azul briefed Stoke whilst his finger indicated the highlighted circular area showing their previous search. "Nothing."

Stoke removed some of the strange vegetation growing on the wall next to them and opened his four-way mouth. The Reptans' diet surprisingly did not contain meat; they had only acquired a taste for moist greens. Stoke contentedly chomped the stuff before swallowing his new found snack - it quenched his thirst and satiated his hunger.

Ignoring him, Zulu was glancing around here and there, building a picture of the scale of the structure in his mind. It was hard enough amongst the darkness of the place, but the extravagantly designed walls and pillars made it almost impossible to find a direct route. *Maybe the Fera liked getting lost,* he chortled before scratching his bottom jaw and turning his gaze back to Azul, who was about to bring bad news…

"Anything on the second duo of scouts?" Stoke asked. It was killing him to find out how their situation had progressed.

Azul shook and lowered his head slightly,

"No battle report has come through yet," he replied abruptly.

Stoke clenched his mighty fist and slammed it into the hieroglyph carved wall, crumbling it under his solid knuckles. *DAMN!*

He withdrew his fist before he launched again. He was stopped mid-way as Azul's grip snapped round his wrist like a clamp.

"Calm down and control yourself!" Azul ordered firmly, releasing Stoke's wrist from his powerful grasp.

Stoke breathed heavily, accepted his orders and banished his frustration. He looked around at his troops who were too busy either searching the vicinity or engaged in petty conversation, pretending not to notice his anger. For this he was thankful - he did not want to let them see he was 'hot headed', even if they were merely pretending not to.

"Now, Arbus has issued orders to continue our search and that's what we're going to do. Understand?" Azul waited expectantly.

There was a brief moment of anticipation.

"Yes, your excellence, forgive my… recklessness," Stoke exhaled.

● ● ●

Anta Margul traversed the length of the rocky cliff-side, his reports held close to his furry chest. It was this Bigadon's mission to update HQ on the work of their sworn enemies, the Gatheren. On arrival the alien race had caused dismay amongst his people – their last known encounter had resulted in the orbital bombardment and destruction of an entire home-world. Such an act would never be forgiven…

He nimbly leapt across the rocks and boulders that governed the landscape. He was nearing the point where Gatheren activity was supposedly in full operation. Apparently they were proceeding with a massive excavation programme – it was his purpose to find out what exactly they were looking for.

The 'primitive' Bigadons were a kindly and amiable species, yet the Gatheren, or 'evil people' as they were referred to by the occupants of the Plaza, the largest Bigadon settlement, were intent on suppressing them.

He picked up the noise of plasma cutters in operation not far away. *At last,* he thought, and scuttled into the shadows. Already he could see translucent-armoured figures on the horizon – no doubt the dreaded soldier Reptans. Fearful of any closely-stationed scouts, he withdrew his sidearm – a weapon developed from the human military technologies they had allowed the Bigadons to replicate, as a means to defend themselves.

And to pursue their own intents and purposes…

He leaned closer, alert. The cliff overhang would provide him with sufficient cover for now, but if he was going to get a closer look at their operation without being killed, he was going to have to be inventive. He doubted that the Gatheren would suspect that a solitary Bigadon would dare spy on them. Both sides knew a single-unit trespassing was more than foolish. If they sighted him, they would have his head. He just prayed he wasn't stupid enough to be found.

The whole picture of what they had been up to was just a few feet ahead. If he could only catch a glimpse – but return home in one piece too? That didn't seem likely.

Probing and electronic spying equipment would be detected and hijacked immediately – the Gatheren had EMP pylons ready to fire at any given second.

For a minute he seemed stumped.

Until he remembered that he could do everything required of him without leaving the cover that the overhang provided him with, by reflection. He reached for his shoulder-pack, undid the rough fastenings and gripped five mirrored plates. He placed each one around the cliff-side, making sure they were going to give him the best view possible. In a minute he had successfully obtained a mirrored image of the excavation going on below, precisely in the region that he dared not enter.

He stared into the shiny blackness, deeper into the shadows, spellbound. A pyramid glowed in the darkness.

Chapter XV
What Lies Beneath

"There have been rumours that the Gatheren have taken an interest in this place," the governor explained as he sent a co-ordinated map directly to Starna's ship. The resourceful Bigadon infiltrator cared little about Gatheren presence – she knew the risks when she had taken up the assignment. She stroked her furrowed brow and frowned.

"I'm not sure I'll be able to come out alive, but I promise I'll do my best," was the only response she could muster. "If the worst comes to the worst and the Gatheren are there, we've always got the humans to help us."

"We can't overlook the possibility that they will be preoccupied with other things. Briefing terminated." The governor's brutish face was gone from the monitor in an eye-blink.

"Report to databank," she said subconsciously, making no effort to steady her nerves whilst giving the report. She did not want to mask the reality of what she was going through.

"Touch-down in five minutes." She played around with the dials and switches, adjusting the blockage on the background-noise. Her hands swept across the controls gracefully, pulling levers and tapping buttons as she kept careful watch on her aircraft's status. Ahead was a chance to discover a lost civilisation, buried deep within a mountain. It was not known if the Gatheren had an active excavation facility running here. The structure was uncovered when a massive landslide caused the mountain top to collapse, revealing the front half of a huge pyramid.

It was her job, a solitary infiltrator, to see what she could find inside.

Close behind were two environment-specialist Bigadons, piloting vessels similar to the one she flew – both were itching to run routine checks on the ancient building, perhaps even more-so than she was to explore it.

Heme and Creed prepared for landing. Starna lowered the nose of her craft accordingly and the three vessels came to a halt within a safe distance of the mountainous wreckage. Huge rocks were scattered across the terrain around them, as far as the eye could see. When her viewpoint changed and she exited her craft, she could ponder over the anomaly. At last they could confirm that there was something here worth having a closer look at. The crystal structure shone eerily under the light of the sun.

Heme and Creed gathered their scientific equipment into a sturdy steel case and followed her lead, muttering in high spirits about possible findings among themselves. They were good company, and she was lucky to have such accomplished workers joining her on this assignment.

"Starna?" Heme asked, his small voice taking on an inquisitive tone.

"Yes?"

"Crede was wondering if we could join on your first-way-round investigation of the interior."

"Sorry, I've been given specific orders to do the first run myself. I am armed, you are not. I've got to look for any potential hazards." Crede had difficulty hiding a deflated look. She didn't like having to dash their hopes in such a way, but how would she look if she allowed them entry, defenceless, if it turned out to be a death-trap?

"Look, I'll try not to damage anything inside, if that's what you're worried about. I'm not about to waste my ammunition in a hurry." She saw that they did not draw much comfort from her words. "Wow." Both Heme and Creed looked up with anticipation. Neither was discouraged at the sight. "Looks like we're here."

Satisfied, Anta gathered the mirrored plates and hastily stowed them away in his shoulder pack. When he reached for the final plate, an explosion ripped the air above him and it shattered before his eyes. Fire crisped his fur and the ground beneath him cracked and gave way, turning to rubble. Before he could help himself he suffered a battering of rock and earth, and then became swallowed in the debris. In a state of shock, he tried to free himself, to no avail. He panicked – what if he was trapped here forever? His last hope was his tracking device – it would send a distress signal with his co-ordinates if he hadn't moved within the hour. Luckily, the Gatheren wouldn't be able to decipher the signal – the comm. systems of other races were still a mystery to them.

Down in the excavation site the barrel of a gun drone smoked after obliterating half of the cliff-side. A Reptan stalker adjusted his magnification emplacement to confirm the kill. He briefly scanned the targeted area, content with finding no survivors.

Chapter XVI

Within the Depths

John and Catriona found themselves in a cold isolation. Thrown into a single cell, they had only just remembered the brutish manner in which they had been captured, *again*. But this time, their captors were not mere greedy humans. They were alien, like the Bigadons, but harbouring far darker intentions.

As John's senses were brought into focus he could vaguely make out the subtle thuds of a by-passer's feet.

He felt an icy chill rise up his spine when he recognised the figure was one of *them*.

The alien's flowing movement gave the impression that it was on guarding duty as it slowly marched by, unaware of John's watchful eyes observing it. As the figure slipped out of sight John diverted his attention to the only companion he had had for days. Catriona stirred, making noise. Her eyes pulled open with great difficulty.

"Where are –" John clasped his hand over her mouth, not wanting to draw the attention of the lurking beast patrolling the premises. Catriona could not help herself from screaming when she saw the creature advancing towards their cell.

Rocketing through space, the *Alpha One* was on a steady course for Pharsee - inside the Alpha Team gazed through the viewing port at the captivating planet. Trooper Brown brought the ship down and executed a sharp left turn, narrowly avoiding an oncoming asteroid. He let out a quick boastful laugh whereas the other members breathed a deep sigh of relief after having just evaded certain death.

"Am I good or what?" he questioned his fellow members.

"That depends on your definition of 'good'," Adaman remarked nervously as he clung to the back of the lead piloting chair where Calron was seated.

Calron tried fiendishly to conceal the expression of amusement that broke through every time he looked at his bewildered comrades.

The soft sound of pistons struggling to manoeuvre a robotic hide broke the silence.

C.R.A.P. (Controlled Responsive Assisting Pilot) moved forward, small shoots of steam emitting from the two chimney-like devices on the robot's head. The knee-high machine strolled along unaffected by the ever-changing simulated gravity, ignorant of his poor form and rusty shell.

"Don't you think you should get a clean up?" Trooper Brown said, as he pulled at the many levers on the control panel.

"Watch that asteroid cluster!" Adaman called, pointing at a group of rocks on a collision course with their ship.

"I got it," he called out, and yanked the foremost of the levers, elevating their craft to a safe position.

C.R.A.P. hit the roof and dropped unperturbed to the deck. He then shot past Tank, before regaining his footing on the steel floor.

"I think it's about time I helped." He strolled to the small alcove designed for his insertion, and uploaded his piloting programming to aid Trooper Brown's navigation through the asteroid belt. From what the little robot was witnessing, Trooper Brown's actions were becoming more hazardous by the minute.

The trio of Bigadons, Starna at the lead, had now neared the entrance to the pyramid. Desperate to investigate, Heme and Crede ushered Starna forward until they were mere feet away from the immaculate walls of the structure.

"Hurry, if you can," Heme said, as he collected the scientific equipment. Creed began assembling various parts of their small testing devices.

"We can do basic tests on the exterior for the best part of a day," Creed explained as he fiddled with different bits and pieces. "But we'll have to wait for the results. If you do the first sweep before sunset, we might get some of the interior done too." Starna nodded in comprehension. She stepped onto the solid crystal floor, anxious to see what was inside the ancient structure.

Anta tried to shift amongst the rubble to ease his discomfort. What little light shone through the cracks and holes of the rubble gave him hope. He heaved under the pressure of hundreds of small rocks. He was in the most dreaded situation possible- calling out for help would only result in the 'evil people' discovering his presence - the last thing he wanted to do. But if he stayed quiet, there was a high possibility that no-one would find him. He pondered over the two options and decided he'd lie low. For now.

A moment when the light ceased to exist was all that was needed to bring him back to a state of alert. A large silhouette dropped past his view, shutting out the sun's rays for all but a second. Anxious to know who or what it was, he struggled to gain a better view from which he could see whatever had just eclipsed him in the darkness. The earth gave way and gradually stronger light hit on his battered face as the rubble pinning him to the ground broke away - enough for him to see who it was. He was thankful he didn't call for help. The heavier rubble atop was irreplaceable.

Down in the excavation site the silhouette turned out to be a figure of the utmost hatred and misfortune to any Bigadon who could remember… Anta felt no privilege in being the first of his kin to see the Gatheren leader. He watched open-mouthed as the eleven foot being moved with inhuman grace around the excavation dig. The new arrival engaged in quick conversation with the Reptan scout accompanied by the diligent gun drone that had trapped Anta – although they thought he was dead. Only time would tell if the drone could truly claim the latter.

Arbus' body burned with rage before he tilted back and roared-

"Any opposition shall be crushed!"

Hearing the declaration Anta paused in fear.

Moments later it leapt almost six feet in the air and vanished into the depths of the pyramid below.

Catriona did not dare touch the security beams for fear of losing a limb – or worse, the possibility of death. She could not be too careful amidst this industrial alien habitat, despite the fact that she was confined to a single cell. Each cold night, she prayed that someone would come and free her and her companion. Only John was keeping her sane for now – she hoped they would never be kept close together long enough for their interest in each other to cease.

But John was strange, in the manner that he was not like any human she had met. He told her tales of his forgotten past, faint memories that he was not even sure he had. He told her of his bewilderment when he first appeared onboard the Horizon – and the horrific events that followed. He could recall things from his 'past', simple things like cars and boats, but could not remember what relevance they had to his forgotten life. At first, when he had only begun telling her tales of his mysterious life, she had considered him a lunatic, a madman of sorts. But he told his tale to her with a strange kind of honesty, and sometimes she almost found herself believing what he said.

In the confines the malevolent aliens had created, she had but one pursuit to keep her occupied – who was this man, and what was he doing here?

As the Gatheren search squad delved deeper into the pyramid, illumination belts were strapped around the bodies of the Tortan species in order to make life easier for the others. They were some of the largest and most dangerous creatures held within the Gatheren ranks. They took on the appearance of large three legged beetles; their elliptic heads bore an armoured strip 'wrapped' round the front for additional protection. Armed with either their deadly machetes or shield formed fists, they became all the more terrifying when Toxicans were mounted in large laser cannons atop their shells, which were similar to that of the howler aircraft. What made the Tortans so unique to the Gatheren was found in their history. In the ancient days of the uniting of the Gatheren, their race was dwelling on a rocky planet later proclaimed Torta. There they lived in peace, oblivious to all other matters concerning the galaxy… that was until the *others* came. Reptan warriors ensnared the beings, believing they could be tamed. What began as a mission to bring Tortans under the rule of the council soon neared the point of escalating into a war. As the final weeks of the battle were drawing near a group of Reptan soldiers became trapped inside a rocky cliff-face that had broken apart and collapsed on top of the group. Their fellow kin tried desperately to free them, seeking out any possible means to do so. However their oxygen was running out fast. The muffled static voices of their own kind communicating below urged the Reptan warriors to work as long as their bodies could endure. Congregating from nearby posts, more joined in the rescue, but not even with all their combined might and speed removing the rubble were they going to reach the survivors buried below. Tortans watched from afar at their efforts and rather than rejoice they felt pity for all the bloodshed and death that had befallen the planet. This was the moment where the Tortans became part of the Gatheren council, gliding over the rocky cliff-face, using their ability of hovering for which the Reptans had sought them out, they joined in the dig. What would have taken days, and inevitably ended in failure, took only hours with the aid of the Tortans in uncovering the survivors. As the last warriors were pulled from the rocky grave that hungered for them, below the battle for Torta was over. Tortans were to become an everlasting part of the Gatheren from then on, sharing a special bond with their Reptan masters who now treated them with respect as well as kindness, looking after and tending to all their needs. Tortans brought along with them their fallen comrades and allowed the Gatheren to utilise their bio-engineering and create the gravity-engine – the basis for all their vehicles. Tortans thought of it as a memorial for the members of their family who fell in the conflict and assured themselves that their lives had not been wasted, for the remainder of their species had ensured the survival of their race for millennia to come...

Marching through the large chambers of the Water Temple, the search squad came to a halt as they reached the enormous doors. Stoke sidled past the Tortans, patting one as he went by. He placed a firm hand on the doors and with a slight push they creaked open. Inside sand and dust dropped over his armoured head like a light blanket. He shook it off and ordered the rest of his squad to follow through. Inside were more cracked tiles, broken pillars and soot littering the floor. He peered onwards, his eyes following collapsed sections of the walls, right down to the ground. As the Tortans moved inwards, what he thought was more rubble slowly formed into the murky remains of some creature that had lived here. He noticed it held a cup that had worn over the millennia, and what was left of its clothing was now nothing more than torn rags. Strangest of all, it struck him to see that it was headless; he followed a trail from the neck bone across the ground and there lay the skull, its mouth wide open, still exhibiting a look of fear. It must have had a gruesome death. The Fera...

• • •

Starna pushed the huge resistant entrance doors aside, Heme and Crede waiting excitedly behind her. "I'll move in and check for any potential threats," she said as the doors illusively seemed to reconfigure themselves under the gaze of Rako, the huge sun which stared down on Pharsee.

"Can you see anything?" Heme asked loud enough for her to hear as she gazed around the derelict and beautiful hall, which so far held no obvious threat.

"You can come in and see the entrance for yourself," she said, staring dumbstruck at the massive shrine in front of her. "Just stay behind me until I'm sure this place is safe."

She could hear the spark of excitement the invitation seemed to have triggered.

"Great, we'll keep behind." She had found a way of entry already, and was mentally prepared to explore further into the temple. The shrine, held in place high above the tiled floor, dominated the entrance chamber. Starna felt insignificant before it – she was but a tiny being compared to its majesty. She was daunted by the looming pillars that overshadowed her.

With a new awareness she moved in for a closer and more detailed analysis. Tiny markings were semi-apparent so she prised away the settled dust and sand to reveal an entire hieroglyph- *was everything here so elaborately detailed*? All tension and unease was gone when she claimed the hall safe, allowing her two eager companions to move around freely.

Wandering forward to the pedestal in the centre of the shrine, Starna looked upon the crystal wall stationed behind it, hoping to find something more to interest her – there was no indication of how to move into the structure. She had met a dead-end.

The outside light found its way upon the complex dial on the pedestal, reflecting onto strange hieroglyphs uncovered on the walls, engraved at angles around it.

She waited patiently for Heme and Crede to catch up with her, their wondrous expressions signifying that they had busied themselves with their studies already, just inside the huge crystal doors.

She called them over to the dial– if anyone alive knew how it worked, it would be Heme or Crede who had the best idea.

Their shadows wavered over behind her – they waddled forward, carrying their heavy equipment. When they saw the dead-end at the far side of the chamber they exchanged glances.

"What is it?" Starna asked amidst the gloom. The structure had been warm on entrance, yet a cold breeze seemed to spread forth from the decorated walls.

"This is the place," Heme said to Crede who nodded in agreement.

"What are you two on about now?" Starna asked, a puzzled stare fixing on her face. "Come on – I'm getting stiff from all this idleness." The two of them wandered forward as if dreaming.

"We'll take care of this, Starna," Crede remarked subconsciously, as he savoured his first taste of the legendary shrine.

"Just as I thought," Heme muttered aside his companion. "We are in the Fire Temple. We've been tracing the hieroglyphs from entry – according to them, this is a Riddle Room."

"I'm not here to solve riddles," Starna replied, clearly uninterested, "though I'm bound to try if it means getting the job done. Do we have any clues?"

Crede approached the ornate dial.

"Well if I have a good look at this maybe we'll find something to help us." He touched the dial as if it were a thing of extreme delicacy – it proved far sturdier that he predicted. He turned one point left: nothing. Then two points left: nothing. Three points left: suddenly an illuminated panel shone a fiery red on the tiled floor. "We've got something! Who's the genius?" Heme exclaimed excitedly. He proceeded toward the glowing panel, as if no obstruction was too great for him to overcome in his fit of excitement.

"Stop!" Starna shouted when she noticed his foolhardy advance. He halted instantly at her command. "You don't know if it may hurt you."

"I'm not too sure our ancestors would try and kill anyone and everyone who would visit them."

"You can't be sure of that." She dropped a seed-pod onto the panel – there was no unexpected reaction – it merely hit the panel and remained inanimate.

"Looks safe to me," Heme said as he placed his foot upon it. Before Starna could intervene, the pyramid shook violently– at the far side of the chamber, behind the pedestal, a section of flooring suddenly sunk inwards, becoming a deep stairway.

Another shower of sand passed over them.

"Ahh, the Lower Levels," Crede uttered under his breath. "Perhaps you should declare it safe before me and my companion proceed."

Ruffled by the sudden change in the architecture, Starna moved past the pedestal and slowly began to tread down the hidden stairway. She wiped away the dust that had settled on her head and shoulders and straightened herself.

The stairway seemed to go on forever, as if forbidding her progress. It was dark and the air was thick. Almost giving up hope after a deep descent down into the abyss, at last a solid stone double-door came into view.

She pulled out her walkie-talkie and reported into it:

"I've made it to the end of the stairway – and not a moment too soon by the looks of it – there's only an hour left until sunset."

"We've got all the supplies we need to stay here a week if need-be. You don't have to hurry. Crede and I will run more tests in the entrance chamber until you give us word to proceed further. Take care."

She placed her hand on the stone door. It had accumulated a great amount of dust – it almost appeared as if it had never been used, for reasons she was about to find out, if only she could find a way to get through it. There was no telling how thick it was from its outward appearance, but it looked built to withstand heavy damage.

Two hours later and she had still not found out how to open it. She had scanned every inch of its outward-construction, had used all the conventional invasive equipment in her small arsenal – she had even used her defensive weaponry to try and bust the lock, but the doors seemed invincible. She had consulted Heme and Crede, and they had promised her that they would help at sunrise the next day. Aware of her long climb back up to her companions, she set off, but could not help but be slightly disheartened by her lack of progress.

When she returned to the entrance chamber, tired after her endless attempts at opening the door, Heme and Crede were waiting patiently, still engrossed in the routine testing of the components of the Temple. The panel that had once shone fire-red was now an indistinguishable tile in the flooring once again.

Suddenly the powerful smell of smoke and soot caught

in their nostrils. Heme and Crede sniffed distastefully around them. Crede began to speak.

"What could possibly be burning in a Temple made almost entirely of cryst –"

He froze, a look of alarm crossing his hard-set features. Immediately he turned to run, and in his haste shouted,

"THE CRAFT! SOMEONE HAS SET FIRE TO OUR CRAFT!" Starna's heart skipped a beat and she felt as though her air supply had been cut off. She wanted to hyperventilate – it was the first time she had been truly frightened since they had touched down near the Temple – exactly where the fire was.

"Save our supplies!" Heme shouted. Crede appeared too conscious of the threat of death to try himself.

Starna rushed for her ship– she had loaded a fair amount of food before the expedition, which she was determined to save. The flames consuming the aircraft contrasted with the starry night sky.

Casting open the boot, the soot began to choke her, but she forced herself to begin unloading– an explosion somewhere behind her claimed Crede's vessel. Shrapnel was cast everywhere and narrowly missed her – Heme had already unloaded the rations aboard his craft, and after throwing them to Crede rushed over to help Starna.

Aware that she had already pushed her time and luck, she urged them back to the Temple, where they took cover from the ensuing explosions in the entrance chamber.

After staring horrified at their ships they looked in dire hope at the pile of food they had gathered at great risk to their lives, which they stowed away at the far corner of the chamber until they hungered. Stranded in the middle of a mountainous, endless terrain, the two scientists recited their religious oaths to the open air.

Starna remained firm and retained her composure, but

Heme and Crede both knew that she was praying inside for all their sakes.

● ● ●

The night became deathly quiet. They had securely shut the Temple doors in an effort to thwart whoever was pursuing them.

"Look, I don't know about you but I'm not going to get any sleep. This place is… bad, that's all I can tell. And the sooner we find another way out of here the better. I'm going to do something useful with this time and have another look at that door. As far as I'm concerned the passage down there is completely safe, but if you would prefer not to take my word for it you're welcome to wait here."

"I'll go," a rasp and almost reluctant voice offered in response. Starna was surprised to see Crede, previously too petrified to do anything after seeing their ships ablaze, volunteering for the task. "I should never have left you two to get the supplies on your own. For that I offer you my service until you are done with me. I can only say I am sorry."

"And so am I," Starna replied. "If I hadn't chosen to go on this assignment then perhaps you two wouldn't have been asked to come along. I feel indebted to you both. Now let's just get out of here. I don't want to spend any more time here than necessary."

"I'll come too," Heme offered, unable to rest in the ancient building – his thirst for discovery was still running strong despite recent events.

"Great – all three of us – the more the merrier. At least we're protected from whoever or whatever is trying to strand us here."

On their journey down the staircase, Starna made

conversation with her two unnerved companions to ease the tension as best she could.

"So, how old is this building, exactly? Did you find anything of interest in your studies?"

"We'll have to send our samples to the lab for the proper results, but from the natural degradation of the walls and floor I'm guessing that we're talking millennia. We found a small compartment on the inside of the dial with three tiles placed like clockwork – they've been operating faultlessly for a long, long time. Two of the tiles have circles on them, and one had an x. We are still unsure of what purpose they serve in this... place," Heme said, hesitating before finishing the sentence. Crede remained silent.

"Not much longer now," she assured them. They had been walking for just under an hour, and their lack of sleep was beginning to wear them down as they had set out in the small hours of the morning. They became alert again only when the stone doors came into sight.

When she saw that they were open, a mixed feeling of fear and confusion penetrated the curtain of fatigue that hung over her, getting heavier by the minute.

"It appears your 'immovable' door has just shifted," Heme said, trying unsuccessfully to mask his unsteady voice. "But perhaps that is not a good thing."

"You two wait here," Starna ordered, ignoring the comment.

"Something is happening in this place and I don't like it."

"I'm coming," Crede replied, suddenly snapping to attention.

"I've abandoned you once before – I won't do it again."

"You have no means of defence – if something springs on you you're finished. I've been given orders which I intend to follow."

"I'm going with you, like it or not. Do me for obstruction or whatever, but I have every right to know what's down there as soon as you do," Crede said defiantly. He was still shaking.

Chapter XVII
The Conquest System

General Gargant of the HAF (Human Alliance Forces) stroked the stubble that protruded from his firm square chin. Twiddling his chain of status between his large fingers, he briefly scanned the panels that formed part of his desk. Accompanying him was Private Strome, a military strategist rising up through the ranks of the HAF military.

The stylus tapped the panel in a staccato fashion. Private Strome remained silent, awaiting his report for his year of service.

"Impressive," General Gargant muttered. "You've stayed well within the boundaries the HAF have imposed during your service." The room was humid, and the interior dim.

The stylus snapped.

"Mass-produced things these days," Gargant grumbled, as he pulled forth the top drawer of his desk and withdrew another, identical to the first. He set aside the broken one, although it seemed unlikely that he would bother to repair it. Strome was under the impression that the man's service was too important to spend time musing over such petty details.

There was an interruption as a voice call was received on his desktop radio. Gargant flipped the receiver switch and listened attentively.

"Important message regarding the Horizon cruiser, General," a female voice informed him.

There was a lapse in conversation as the General took time to remember the task that had been set for this ship.

"Thank you Sandra," he replied before terminating the channel. He saved the message to the databank.

He brought himself back to the information that lay before him, continuing his examination of Strome's year-record.

"There isn't much more I can add to what I've already said." Strome recognised this as a formal and perhaps even praising dismissal.

Now that the brief meeting had been brought to a close Private Strome began to download his report from the General's desk. No longer paying the private any heed, the General altered the frequency of the incoming signal. He tampered with the holographic panel at the front of his metallic desk, and found the new message. Ignorant of Strome's presence, he pressed play. A holographic image of Captain George Cameron Band of the Horizon cruiser jittered into action. The Captain's face was drawn – signs of overworking were all too apparent on his aging face.

"I am sending a request to all nearby HAF stations to deploy large-scale military forces to the new-found planet Pharsee if the captives, including my daughter and a civilian named John (file enclosed), are not found in due course. I also request aid for the Horizon, which has taken damage from a recent terrorist incursion. The vessel is holding half a million people. Although the fleet has broken off, taking cover in Pharsee, our ship will take at least a week to abort to the nearest HAF station – longer depending on how the evacuation of the human populace on Pharsee goes. Transmissions from the sophisticated native race, the Bigadons, have been established. Evacuation of humans on Pharsee will begin in unison with the collection of my daughter and the civilian she is believed to be in the company of. On an additional note, there was an unauthorised MPCD placed onboard this ship named Tank Mark 2. I leave all information regarding these specific incidents via encrypted document." *END OF MESSAGE...*

Gargant found taking in all this information a daunting task, as several aspects of recent events played on his mind. Tank Mark 2? The name seemed to ring inside his head, as if it were relevant to recent goings-on. The door shut discreetly behind him. A strange Icon appeared on his data-tab.

DOWNLOAD COMPLETE
- From George Cameron Band regarding subject 'John'. Identified surname: **Spader.**
- Origin – **UNKNOWN.**

Starna guided her companions into the small enclosure. They eagerly followed her along the dim corridor to an unknown end– she could sense that the climax to their efforts was at hand.

She had undone the safety on her firearm as a precaution, though she was under the impression that no threat could have endured millennia of entrapment within the ancient walls.

"What do you think could be down here? I wonder what the Pharseeans are hiding," Heme whispered to Crede in an obvious effort to steady the Bigadon's failing nerve. The Bigadons always called their ancestors the 'Pharseeans', though there were arguments that they were actually called the 'Fera'.

"It- it couldn't be anything dangerous – nothing could have lived down here for this long… could it Heme?"

Ignoring the senseless mutterings of the two scientists, Starna crept the length of the corridor, her small flashlight drawing exaggerated lines across the crystalline walls.

The moonlight reflected down the length of the pyramid, so that even the low levels were still tainted with an icy glow.

Starna edged her way along the corridor, denying herself the urge to run around the bend haphazardly to kill the tension.

The two scientists stuck to her like a sibling does to its mother in times of danger – Crede was reluctant to stray from between his two more-courageous companions and was insistent on remaining in the middle, the position which he no doubt thought was the safest.

Starna took it upon herself to be the first to seek out any potential threats, fulfilling her primary purpose in the group. She pulled out from behind the dark corridor and stared down the barrel of her weapon, but she could see little through the darkness. Ahead was the suggestion of more footwork – another room or corridor was linked to the one that she stood in, or so was her first impression.

"We're not there yet," she confirmed to Heme and Crede, both of whom looked as though they would rather be anywhere else; so much so that Starna was actually surprised at how terrified they seemed, as if the very dark that surrounded them was in reality instruments of torture.

"Are you two sure you wouldn't rather wait on the stairwell?" she was feeling generous enough to give them the chance to opt out, no matter how much their reactions so far had driven her to go further.

Crede seemed to be seriously considering the suggestion, but a few subtle and encouraging nudges from his fellow scientist reassured him.

"We're fine," Heme answered. "Aren't we, Crede?"

"Ye – yes, we are. I don't know what came over me. This could be the lead up to the most important archaeological find in centuries," he replied, seeking assurance from his comrades.

"If you say so. I'm moving up ahead." Starna lowered her weapon and directed the flashlight further down the corridor. Her suspicions were proved correct when the beam pushed ahead through the dark and into a second enclosure. "Yup – more up ahead. So who's going first?" she asked jokingly and swept the torch onto the faces of her fellow explorers. Heme at least tried to forge a smile in an effort to hide his fear. Crede's complexion turned sickly under the light and looked as if he were about to die. Their furry faces were beaded with sweat.

"Don't all jump at once," Starna mused as she broke off from the formation they had kept since they entered the 'Lower Levels'. She didn't need to try hard to stay calm, even when she noticed another descent down a stone ramp-way, where even the moonlight could not reach. She had had far worse experiences of dark areas - where real threats existed.

"I hate to tell you – we're going down again." This time there was only silence from her normally responsive company.

"Come on. We've been in here longer than any of us would have liked now anyway." She led them into the pitch darkness, even deeper into the ancient building. Heme and Crede still took interest in examining the architecture of the temple and discussing which myths concerning it were true and which were not.

"It has become well-known in modern mythology that the temple was said to have only two levels. They were wrong in saying that. It's strange how some people 'know' these things even though we're the first to explore the place. I mean it's like they're taking credit for their courage in daring to explore here when they haven't even seen the place – it was buried in a mountain. If nobody's ever been in here then they can't honestly say that what they say is true. They just make stuff up and hope people will believe what they say, and hope that they will be remembered when people tell other people that they were told by the person who they told what they just told the other person, and so the person they're telling will tell others around them of the person who told the person who told them and –"

"Heme, please button it." Crede laughed–an expression that Starna had suspected she wouldn't have heard until they were well away from the cautionary areas they were exploring.

"You're right, I am," he admitted, a smile just visible in the torch-lit, crisp air. Crede gave Heme a playful pat on the back.

"It's ok. We've all been known to ramble on every now and again." They had reached the bottom of the descent into the darkest area of the temple and their heads scraped the roof on entry.

"We're at the bottom. Hopefully we won't have to go any further than down here. You don't know how disappointed I'll be if this place turns out to be empty," Starna added, to portray her feelings before they found out if their efforts were to be rewarded or not. "I mean, it's an honour to be first to rediscover a place and all that, but I'd have been as well putting my energies into something else if there's nothing here."

"Well I can honestly say that this is as good as it gets for me, regardless," Heme admitted as they advanced through the disappointingly empty room. "Although I can't explain how much a big discovery would boost my career." Crede remained silent, occupied by his own thoughts.

At the end of the single small room which an entire level had been devoted to, were three large mirrors, each equal in size to the explorers who stood before them.

"It doesn't look like we've hit the jackpot today, folks," Starna said flatly as she scanned the room with her flashlight, and finding nothing else except the mirrors, she took a deep breath to comfort herself.

"Well, as I said, regardless."

"I do remember something about mirrors, now that I think about it," Crede uttered. "Something about misplacing them to deceive or something." Starna tried lifting the mirrors from their fixed position on the wall but they seemed adamant that they wouldn't be removed by force. She gripped her weapon and slammed the butt into the central mirror which shattered, revealing another passageway ahead.

"How do you come up with things like that?" She asked rhetorically, immediately recognising the discovery as another opportunity to recover something of value from the heavily funded expedition. "Let's move," she advised and set foot upon the hidden ground. A ghastly fog had settled on the cold stone foundation of the flooring. The mist seemed to have appeared on contact, and Starna was the only one taking notice of it. She thought it best to keep quiet for now – alerting Heme and Crede was the last thing on her to-do list, as she was the only one who really needed to keep an eye out anyway, and they relied on her for protection.

The flashlight failed to spear through the mist that rose ahead, and her two unsettled companions began to show signs of doubt again.

"It's ok," she reassured them. "As long as I'm up front, nothing bad will come of you two."

The pair of scientists merely smiled in return, but she could see that they still needed reassurance.

"I'll move up ahead alone if you like."

"If you insist," Crede replied.

She palmed her secondary firearm, a small and less-efficient armament than her standard one, to Heme, who accepted it out of good manners.

She was beginning to wear down because of her lack of sleep, but she knew that the sooner she had encountered whatever was waiting for her in the darkness ahead the quicker they could begin their journey to the surface where they could rest. Sleep deprivation was common in many of her assignments, but she had found that on high-risk missions the adrenaline had its way of reversing the effects of tiredness. Previous assignments had been dangerous, and in a nut-shell, a lot more exciting. So far she had encountered nothing of interest to her, and began to think that the previous occupants of Pharsee were a lot less adventurous than they were made out to be.

That was, until she saw it, glinting in the darkness, penetrating the cold fog and bathed in light. A pentagonal crystal, as large as her head, fixated to a stone pedestal – at that moment all her doubts were washed away, the curtain of fatigue demeaning her grace lifted. The majesty of the stone left her speechless – many seconds passed while she tried to summon enough strength to call to her comrades whom, she knew, would be delighted at the find.

Chapter XVIII
First of many

It had been a good half hour in the temple and the Gatheren search squad were making progress by the minute. To his delight, Stoke had not only discovered some pedestal that lay dormant in the far off section of the chamber but also managed by some means or another to operate the ancient device. With a slight twist, the circular plate embedded in the pedestal gave way with minimal resistance and rotated three clicks to the left before stopping. Unexpectedly, a tiled part of the ground near the leader became a watery blue incandescence, arousing excitement throughout the squad. Ragal approached the leader and slapped Stoke's back. He chortled at the gesture.

"Watch, the wall moves, it beckons our search. I swear even the spirits of the Fera believe in our goals. Arbus will be most honoured if we find that which we search for."

"Indeed he will – 'Any opposition shall be crushed!'" he cheered, quoting their leader. The surrounding squad yelled in delight upon hearing the famous words. With renewed confidence the squad C*2 cautiously moved into the darkness of the staircase. With the Tortans up front their journey would not be as treacherous down the blackened interior beyond. Glancing at the details on the walls as he went by, Stoke noticed what would have probably been the holdalls for lights or perhaps what the Gatheren had recently discovered; the crystal shards the Fera used to combat the darkness and their dreaded enemies – the OverCast themselves. What really caught his attention however, was the fact that a lot of the artefacts were in rather good condition for being shut off from all for so long. Sure, there were the collapsed sections of both walls and pillars within the temple, but a lot was just covered in dust or ash, waiting to be rediscovered and, if it was the same for the gem, then it would be in the Gatheren's possession not long from now.

He nudged Ragal to get his attention.

"What do you believe our lord intends to do with these sacred artefacts?"

Ragal scratched his neck, thinking himself about what Arbus had planned,

"From the word that flows, I've heard it will help us to see our path more clearly, it will unite us in a way that we've never before experienced and bring about the final battle with the creatures."

Stoke pondered on the idea of yet further unity, and the idea of a last showdown with the Mites made him grin. He did not question his leader's intentions as he was merely curious.

The chatter of the surrounding members helped comfort him in a place such as this. Knowing that fellow warriors were nearby helped block out any doubts about the trek, such as traps or beasts that dwelled in shadow. He clenched his fist and recalled that he was a ferocious warrior, who had taken the oath that bound all members of the Gatheren, and even if it did result in death he did not fear it, for his life was purposeful. Dying an unfulfilled and purposeless creature was one of the only things he feared, as most of the other members of the Gatheren would undoubtedly agree.

The staircase seemed to go on forever and now the air had become thick. Dun moaned and complained along with other members of his race but restlessly they carried on.

Unexpectedly a loud clap broke the silence and all other members of the squad turned back to see Chub looking at them in supposed confusion.

"What?" he asked, trying to cover up the digestive noises coming from his rear.

Fellow Toxicans burst out in a fit of laughter and even a few Reptans sniggered at the little being. Toxicans did originate from a gas based planet and were therefore prone to making these absurd noises. Dun laughed so hard he stumbled about and lost his footing. He fell down several steps and disappeared into shadow before thudding against a solid object. Tortans picked up pace to see what had happened to the little Toxican, causing the rest of the group to follow quickly to avoid being left in the dark. On arrival they found Dun picking himself up and brushing off the dust that covered his atmosphere suit. Shaken by the tumble, his many tentacle legs wiggled as he raised his head to see what he had bumped into. A large door encrypted with the same hieroglyph they had encountered previously, in the corridor above, was barely visible. Cracks ran across the chamber door, verging in and out of the carved symbol giving it an even greater look of age. Shifting aside Dun, Stoke brushed his hand across the door, revealing the symbol in greater detail. He pushed with increasing pressure but it did not budge. Ragal and two other Reptans attempted to aid his struggle but still the door stood there, an immovable object blocking their path. He slapped the wall in disgust and stepped back. Raising his hand he pointed two large fingers at the door, signalling for the Tortans. Reptans stood aside to let the creatures do what they did best. They chook uncontrollably for a brief moment, building up their strength.

"Destroy that barricade!" Stoke ordered.

Unleashing their anger, the beetle-like aliens smashed and sliced the heavy door apart, piece by piece. Kicking up dust from the assault, the Reptans coughed to clear their three lungs, whilst the Toxicans took shelter behind their superiors from the chunks of debris that were getting catapulted all over the place. The smashing of rock echoed up the stairwell, yet the Tortans continued. Stoke scratched his arm, waiting contentedly as he watched the aliens gradually break the door down. Spears of light shone through the cracks as the Tortans dismantled the door, and soon enough the final chamber came into view. Reptans leapt inside, their honour blades active, whirring and humming as they climbed over the levelled rubble. Inside Stoke drank in all he saw; in the middle of the room was a lake of water surrounding a large pedestal which held the treasure they had been searching for. Cheers erupted from the squad as they all entered the chamber and laid eyes upon the sacred item. Stoke contacted commander Azul, informing him of the marvellous news whilst the others found themselves awestruck by the pearlescent blue diamond. Their search for the first crystal was over!

Ragal stood atop a mound of collapsed pillar, gaining his footing as he did so.

"Our lord has guided us here! He knows all, he feels all, and he is the touch of the Gatheren and look at what he has found by leading us here!"

An encouraging memory flowed though the group, increasing their pride and clarifying their vision.

"And let that be the first of many."

They turned their attention to their lord as his magnificent form crouched under the opening of the smashed door before standing erect to face them. He strode through the knee-deep lake towards the jewel and climbed atop the pedestal. Water shimmered against his shins before dripping back into the lake. He placed his large hand over the blue artefact, slowly and delicately removing it from its resting place. Turning around, Arbus roared at this climactic moment,

"Any opposition shall be crushed!"

Cheers and roars from the surrounding squad members filled the air and echoed throughout the large chamber. Arbus marched back through the lake and headed for the surface, clutching the gem in his hand, the search squad in his pursuit.

Behind them they left a now very empty ancient pedestal...

Chapter XIX
The Hidden Treasure

"This is it! The rumours are true!" Crede announced conclusively after a thorough examination of the stone. With help from his co-worker he had managed to remove the gem from the pedestal. "We must bring it to safety immediately," he declared.

"But our ships have been destroyed!" Heme reminded him. "And, while we're on that subject, we still haven't found the culprit!"

"Well, we can't just run out and demand that they escort us back to the Plaza. It's highly unlikely that they'll agree to that."

"Why don't we just start making our way back anyway? There's nothing left here, and lord knows we'll have plenty of time to decide what to do – it takes hours to climb those stairs," Starna suggested.

Heme and Crede began to trot behind her as they paced the winding crystal corridors, their minds and eyes fixed on the mystical treasure to such an extent that Starna had to orally direct them through the dark passageways, and onwards up to the stairs, to stop them bumping into the walls.

The gemstone seemed to be the only thing keeping the two scientists from collapsing in exhaustion – Starna found the journey back up the infinite staircase three times as hard as it had been on the way down.

She took a moment to praise the unfailing technology in the little flashlight that she had fixed to her shoulder-padding. It had not winked out, like it surely would have done in some typical horror fantasy that the humans sometimes spoke about. Horror was not one of the things the Bigadons liked to indulge in – it seemed ridiculous to them to wallow in the fear and eventual fates that ensued the people of their race as the humans so often did, be it fiction or not.

They had scaled a good many stairs in the comfort and safety of the little flashlight, when some evil influence compelled it to loosen from its secure fastening and tumble down behind her, disappearing down the steps before she could even figure out why she had suddenly become consumed by a torrent of darkness.

Heme was aware of the disaster seconds before it happened, but was too busy adjusting his footwork to meet with the torch when it scuttled past him and tumbled down the stone stairway, so far and fast that it winked out, its light lost in the descent that they had just arisen from.

Heme was the first to try and regroup the trio.

"Starna! Crede! Please tell me that you're both OK, because I am *soiling myself*, as the humans would say."

"I'm here," Starna responded, remaining perfectly still on the step where she cursed the loosened straps that held the torch. "And we'll be fine, as long as we stick together." The straps hanging at her side suddenly gave her an idea.

"I'm here too," Crede said uncertainly, as if he was not actually sure.

"Look, we can get through this. We've been here before and we know it's just a normal, if ancient, stairway. If we move slow and steady we'll reach the top within the hour."

"Maybe less of the slow, I'm itching to get out of here," Crede said as he cradled the huge gem in his arms.

"Right… this would be so much easier if we were to do it in the light," she sighed as she moved toward the voice of Crede. "Pass me your shoulder strap."

"What – why?"

"Do it Heme!" Crede ordered, for the first time taking on the voice of authority.

"Ok, ok, here you go." Her fingers fumbling in the darkness, Starna quickly made a rough bond between them, and was swift in doing the same with Crede.

"Now we know if we lose each other. As per usual, I'll lead."

She began to climb the first step ahead of her, the knots she had forged tugging the two scientists behind and forcing them to move together.

So they climbed, and climbed, and climbed through the darkness, all the while cursing the very straps that held them together for letting loose the torch, which was now out of view for ever.

"I wonder if – ow! - slow down," Heme called sharply to Starna, a few steps above him. "I wonder if someone eventually follows the path down there," he continued, "and finds our torch, and discovers that they wouldn't be the first to be down there. I mean, imagine a different race! Take the hated evil people for example."

"I see what you mean," Crede muttered behind him, smoothing his palms against the perfect facets of the ancient treasure.

"There's no telling what will happen in the future," Starna declared assuredly. "Now let's stop talking and concentrate on the walking. The humans will be celebrating a new day by the time we get to the top of these stairs at the rate we're going."

There was a short pause, but Starna could tell that Heme's voice would be the first to break the silence. She was right. She always found it annoying when people were predictable.

"I do wonder what purpose this treasure could serve though. I mean, I'm not too sure why everyone started talking about 'helping the war effort, something something something,' but I don't think we can honestly do much with this rock." He watched it glow softly behind him.

"Do you say everything you think?" Crede asked, as he trailed at the tail end of the chain they had formed.

"The stone might be worth something, you never know," Starna added positively.

"Actually, that phrase is incorrect Starna – there are some things that we do know, otherwise we would probably all be dead by now."

Starna scoffed loudly. There were some people that just couldn't be bettered when it came to pulling her leg.

"If you don't pick up the pace soon, you two, then we'll starve before we get to the top of this staircase. Crede, if the treasure is slowing you down, I'll take the weight off your shoulders, for a while at least."

"Actually, the weight is in his arms," Heme pointed out.

Starna bit her lip.

"No Starna, I'm fine thanks – this thing, surprisingly, weighs next to nothing."

"Good to hear," she said, as she skipped the next few steps in an effort to provoke her dwindling companions into speeding up.

"But not if it demeans its value, as it could very well do." For once, nobody bothered responding to Heme's negative comments.

As they trudged onward, the first signs of the withdrawal of darkness raised their spirits, and with new-found energy they were able to make the last stretch of the staircase without a third break.

They passed the ornate pedestal and moved into the entrance hall, hastily undoing the shoulder bonds holding them together and moved to gather the last of their supplies.

"Wait," Starna ordered hesitantly. "There's no point in carrying this load with us. We'll eat now and then we'll have to find a way to get across hundreds of kilometres on a single meal. Our ships have been destroyed, and without them, we're going nowhere. Our only real option is to signal for help."

"I don't feel like staying here any longer," Heme moaned in dismay, collapsing onto the dusty ground. "My feet ache and there's no way I'm going all the way back to the Plaza on foot, or even trying for that matter. It's an impossible feat anyway."

"I was joking about that part," Starna said icily. "Obviously there's no earthly way we could close that distance on foot with the supplies we have left."

"I'm sure I left a communicator in amongst this," Crede muttered as he set aside the large gem and began raking through their supplies. "Aha – here we are!" he lifted a small broadcasting device in the air and immediately began tampering with it. "Now, I'll have to make the message we send relatively short or audio only, because I'll have to send it on a long wavelength."

"And why is that?" Heme asked Inquisitively, though did not listen to the response.

"Short waves carry more information. Long waves diffract, or bend around obstacles more. Since we're in a mountainous region I'll have to take the benefit of the latter."

"We'll, you're the expert," Starna said, sarcastically.

"I'm the only one here with half a clue of how to use this thing, so unless you want to rely completely on guesswork I suggest you ride along with me. Now… let me see…"

Chapter XX
Double Rescue

"Intercepted incoming signal," C.R.A.P. informed the Alpha Team, as he brought up the signal frequency and immediately began to decode it.

A voice transmission began to play on the command console, and C.R.A.P. adjusted the amplitude until it met the humans' preferences.

"Hello? Is there anybody out there?" The signal was heard by both Adaman and Calron who alerted the others. "It's Crede here, with my two companions, Heme and Starna. Our aircraft have been destroyed as a result of an offensive from an unknown enemy. We have enough supplies to last us a few days but we have no means of getting back to our central population hub. We're located in a mountainous region near a collapsed mountain top, in an archaic Temple built by the previous dwellers of this planet. I've sent our co-ordinates along with this message. If no further progress has been made in the next few hours I will send a second transmission. Please come and find us." The message ended, leaving nothing but static.

"Have you got those co-ordinates yet, C.R.A.P.?"

"Co-ordinates are being uploaded. Should I divert my course to suit a new purpose?"

"If the co-ordinates received are closer to our current position, then yes," Calron answered, after debating the matter with his allies.

"Looks like we'll be saving more than one life today," Trooper

Brown said, as he strolled into the command deck brandishing a metallic flask of KSK Gold.

"Co-ordinates uploaded. I can confirm that the latest co-ordinates received are closer to our current position than the mission currently in progress."

"Divert our course. We'll make this short and sweet and then follow through with our primary objectives. The Captain hasn't given us a deadline to rescue his daughter yet."

C.R.A.P. beeped to confirm he had followed through with Calron's orders.

"New objective has been set. 300km until arrival at new checkpoint – estimated time until arrival: 20 minutes at seventy-five percent ion thrust."

"Wonder what their story is," Trooper Brown mused under the ambient gaze of the overhead lights.

"Well I guess we're about to find out," Calron replied, his face clouding over.

"I broadcast the message fifteen minutes ago. We can't expect to get help for at least another hour. We should just rest until someone arrives to pick us up."

"*If* someone arrives to pick us up," Heme corrected. "And effectively saves us."

"We're not about to die in here," Starna declared determinedly. "And while we're waiting, I'm going to take advantage of this time when I'm at a loose end, take Crede's advice and get some rest. No offence, but carrying your loads as well as mine has me spent," she said, rubbing the area of her leg which had been having spasms since she had had to 'encourage' her companions, as they climbed the infinite staircase. "And, to prepare for the worst, I think we should see what supplies we have and try and make something out of them – a temporary camp if you like. I'll search for my roll-up bed and some pillows – it was a good thing that we came prepared to stay a while."

"And I'll spend some more time examining this portentous gemstone," Crede announced excitedly.

"And I'll laze around complaining until things are back to normal."

"Oh really," Starna disagreed with his attitude. "What is normal anyway? I mean with our ever-changing society and war with alien species and the rest of it... I don't think our people will see 'normal' again for a long time."

There was an awkward silence, a rare thing with Heme as company. A sickly moment washed over them as they remembered the most depressing aspect regarding the nature of their people: they could fight throughout their entire lives, trying to dispel the evils that tainted their home world, but they would never see the time when their people were free of the forces they sought to vanquish.

A noise outside the entrance doors brought such thoughts to an abrupt end – the subtle sound of gushing air, slowly getting louder as a vessel made its descent onto the open plains near the wreckage of their ships.

"Quick – hide!" Starna alerted them as she dashed towards the pedestal at the far end of the chamber and crouched down behind it.

Crede immediately found cover in amongst the large mound of supplies. Heme pretended to be dead, and then realised how vulnerable he would be despite his average acting skills and dived to take refuge beside his fellow scientist.

Starna set the mode on her weapon to 'stun', the closest function to kill, which she could convert to its deadliest effect in an instant if needed.

C.R.A.P. left the engines on standby in case the situation

inside the Temple was critical and an evacuation became necessary. He automatically opened the rear compartment hatch to allow the Alpha Team to depart.

Tank and Slayer bounded from the rear compartment and landed with a grace that seemed alien, especially for Tank, a machine so large and cumbersome he made craters several feet deep on contact with the desert-like terrain below.

Adaman, Trooper Brown and Calron exited swiftly, their minds and weapons ready to meet any threat. The ancient Fire Temple stood before them, beside it a collapsed mountain top just as had been described in the transmission they had received twenty minutes before.

Wasting no time in overcoming the obstruction that stood before him, Tank plummeted into the entrance doors, capsizing them. The Alpha Team were in before the doors had even hit the ground…

Her aim faltering because of the sudden violent commotion that echoed throughout the chamber, Starna quickly cocked her head up above the pedestal she knelt under but alarmingly found she could see nothing through the waves of dust approaching her position from the collapsed entrance doors. As long as she couldn't see the intruders, she had been trained to assume that they were an enemy unless the methods used were recognisable as being those used by her own race.

She had been entrusted with the protection of her two comrades – she was determined that she would not fail.

Two mighty crashes further weakened her resolve, and when she noticed the sheer bulk of one of the invaders she considered taking a different path of action than that of aggression – this thought was dismissed when she realised that she was the only one who could stand up for Heme and Crede, who although were safely tucked away and out of sight, would eventually suffer the full consequences of her actions during these moments.

Her breathing uneven, she forced herself to confront the intruders.

Darting along the entrance hall, her footwork a practiced art, she brought herself within arms range of the juggernaut that stood before her. Dispensing seven stun rounds into its bulk before hastily withdrawing out of range again, dismayingly to no effect, destroyed her morale – the juggernaut began to charge toward her, the stunning rounds fixed onto its mechanical shell.

When she noticed the humans behind it she was almost caught off-guard. She had taken an offensive stance based entirely on their violent entrance and her military protocol. Humans were effectively allies to the Bigadons in many cases. Her judgement, it had become clear to her now, was entirely wrong.

She stopped dead in her tracks, her gaze wandering over the faces of the homo sapiens, seeking out any signs of malicious intent. On order from the armour-clad white-masked human, the juggernaut ceased its advance and withdrew, its hulking shadow withdrawing from over her, leaving the first rays of the outside light kissing her downy skin.

Even the androids did not seem to know what was happening when all of a sudden the light disappeared and a massed gathering of ghastly creatures, resembling violet jellyfish, broke free from the ceiling and dived down towards them.

Calron had given the order for the juggernaut to cease its attack on the Bigadon, and immediately he brought himself to re-issue an offensive on the swarms of glowing creatures descending from above. In the darkness of the chamber he turned to notice that their only exit had been blocked by a shoal of the jellyfish, their silence signifying one thing only – they were hungry.

Tank sent a volley of rockets high in the chamber, nearing the roof; three aligned missiles tore countless of the creatures apart, yet their ranks were filled again almost instantaneously.

Bewildered as the newcomer-humans were, they provided a safety blanket – a certain degree of altitude that they refused to let the approaching swarms invade.

Starna's first instinct was to rally Heme and Crede – if the humans cut through the aliens blocking the entrance they would have to be ready to escape within seconds.

• Starna & Calron •

As the thought crossed her mind she backed to where she remembered the supply stock was placed. The jellyfish-resembling creatures gave off a purple aura, but it was not bright enough to extend more than a foot into the surrounding gloom. Starna experienced the full spectacle of their massed numbers as they floated downwards silently, like purple lanterns.

Her heart froze when she saw the aura beginning to climb up her arms. On turning she found she was less than a foot away from the acidic tentacles of three of the creatures; the rest were still floating downwards. Gunfire tore the air from near the entrance, lances of light arcing into the infested rooftop of the chamber, and panicked shouting of orders could be heard in the short intervals between successive explosions.

Starna adjusted her weapon to kill and pointed the barrel menacingly at the trio of purple beings who continued to advance regardless. She pulled the trigger twice, and the creatures popped, dispersing a sickly pulp that spread everywhere. The last of the trio in striking distance raised its tentacle, a flap opening at the end. She could already see the attack before it had been executed, and flung herself out of range. From inside the creature drew a burst of acidic liquid, spouting it in her direction, yet missing her. Alarmingly she saw the humans start a fresh assault on the ones blocking the entrance, or in this case, the only exit, and she frantically began booting supplies off the top of the stack until she found Crede, whom she dragged out kicking and screaming.

"It's me Crede! We've got to move!" She twisted sharply on the spot and fired at the third jellyfish before it could disperse a second shot of acid at her.

Crede forced himself to open his eyes to the familiar voice.

"Right!" He scuttled along the battle-scarred tiles. "Come

on Heme, MOVE IT! Get the stone!" he remembered, but Starna was already onto it. She quickly disposed of the jellyfish swarming around the crystal, their deaths resulting in increasing darkness spreading through the chamber. Crede's calves in one hand, the gem and her gun in her other arm, she forced herself towards the open swathe the humans had made. Heme ran close behind, his eyes shining brightly under the purple glare of the pursuing monstrosities.

The humans, with the help of their robotic companions, had eliminated the remaining aliens and opened up the exit. The three explorers, with the ancient treasure in hand, stormed out of the entrance.

The human ship had activated its weapon systems and began cutting down the aliens as they passed through the entrance in hungry pursuit of their escaping prey. Chain guns mounted on the sides of the small craft dispensed thousands of rounds of ammunition in an eye-blink, and as the allied peoples made their escape the jellyfish withdrew back into their domain, their hunger still left unsatisfied.

Starna dropped Crede's leg and allowed him to move by his own free will once they had boarded the human craft. She then gave the treasure to him and he stowed it away in a backpack. She moved toward the white-armoured human, grappling the bars above her head to stop herself losing balance during the ships ascent.

"Hello? – human – did you get our distress call?" she said, still panting after her explosive effort to escape.

Calron turned to meet her gaze, his voice amplified through his helmet. When he noticed how close she had got to him he backed away sharply. She actually found the fright she had given him quite funny.

"Yes- we received the signal..." he leaned overhead the command console and checked the objective counter.

"Approximately 28 minutes ago. Please fasten yourselves into the passenger accommodation," he requested of the exploration team.

Heme was the first to try and work the many complex fastenings each space had been provided with. When he could not fathom the function of the various belts and straps, he tied them into a crude knot and was content with that.

Starna and Crede sat silently, helping each other in, before beginning to explain their situation to the humans.

"We give you our full gratitude – we are not ignorant to the fact that those *things*," she said distastefully, "whatever they were, would have been eating us if you hadn't intervened."

"It's what we do," Trooper Brown said in a feigned punchy voice before asking, "Calron, we got any more fast frozen bottled water?"

"It'll be in the supply store," Calron replied automatically, having been used to answering the same question every few days. He then removed the seals around his helmet, lifting it off as a sign of good manners. He had several battle-scars mapped on his youthful face, but his features were set soft and welcoming as well as determined. He swept away the dust and dirt which had accumulated on his armour and ruffled his dark hair.

"Great," Trooper Brown said in thanks. "Do our guests want some? Nothing like a cold glass of water after a frightening ordeal."

"What?" Heme asked, pretending to be interested as always.

"Water – bottled," Trooper Brown explained slowly.

"No thanks," the Bigadon answered before lying back against the comfortable padded recesses of the seat.

"Well, if you want any I'll be in the galley," Trooper Brown offered, dismissing himself.

"This place has a galley?" Starna asked, thinking she had misheard the human.

"Yes – it's small but it has all the necessary components." Calron could tell from the look on her face that she was impressed. "It's nothing to get excited about, I'm sorry to admit – it's little bigger than a box room."

"Humans live in boxes?" Heme asked. He did not get an answer.

"You must be pretty important to have a ship so luxuriously fitted out," Starna replied as she caressed the leather padding of her seat. "Few Bigadon vessels are built to accommodate more that five people – let alone give them kitchen facilities."

Calron blushed, finding it hard to meet the unflinching gaze of the attractive, almost human, alien.

"The purpose of a ship built for war is not to please its occupants – its primary purpose is to withstand damage, whilst at the same time inflicting it on enemy units to maximum effect," Adaman said whilst he worked on the command console, confirming completed objectives and rehearsing the task ahead – they planned to drop the passengers off at the Plaza, the central Bigadon population hub, and follow through with their primary mission at dawn.

"I see – I've only had the privilege of flying in a frigate of this quality once before," she admitted earnestly.

"Well just make the most of it – hopefully your path won't cross with this ship again – it usually means bad news."

"What do you mean by that?" Crede asked, for the first time taking part in conversation with the humans.

"He means that this ship was made to rescue important people who find themselves in situations of extreme danger. And, since there's normally a lot of both to be found on this planet, that's why we're always on the go – it also explains why our ship is accommodated with everyday utilities and comforts," Trooper Brown clarified from the neighbouring room. The sounds coming from there suggested he was preparing a drink for himself.

C.R.A.P. (Controlled Responsive Assisting Pilot) disengaged from the ship mainframe, its auto-steering programming taking the Alpha Team to their next objective just as effectively as his navigation skills could. He wheeled around the small passenger compartment, his internal A.I. finding the new species onboard interesting.

TARGET:

UNKNOWN SPECIES ... UPDATING DATABASE WITH PHYSICAL CHARACTERISTICS FOR FURTHER REFERENCE - WILL MONITOR PERSONAL QUALITES TO LATER MAKE COMPARISONS WITH COMMON HUMAN BEHAVIOUR PATTERNS

Ae:'{{exe.? Jpg htl.}}

Trooper Brown entered the compartment, a chilled cup of water in his hand.

C.R.A.P.'s navigation systems faulted and he accidentally steered into Trooper Brown's knees. The mercenary amusedly lifted the little robot to head-height in order to interact with him.

TARGET:

HOMO SAPIEN

NAME:

TROOPER BROWN

DETAILS:

MERCENARY EMPLOYED BY EARTH MILITARY, ASSIGNED MEMBER OF ALPHA TEAM, SPECIALISES IN ELIMINATION OF HOSTILE ALIEN SPECIES

PERSONAL CHARACTERISTICS:

ATTEMPTED HUMOUR PROVED TO BE UNSUCCESSFUL IN MANY CASES, OCCASIONALLY IRRITATING, CONSTANTLY INTTERUPTING

PHYSICAL CHARACTERISTICS:

TALL, BROWN, [TIME WEARING HELMET COMPARED TO TIME WITHOUT HELMET [RATIO 3:1]

STATUS:

MUST ESCAPE FROM GRASP

IF CURRENT STATUS EXCEEDS 15 SECONDS TO THE NEXT MINUTE, SHUTDOWN ADVISED

Ae:'{{exe. configured]status..] Hjl_log = no.K18.}}

• Trooper Brown •

"This guy needs a clean-up," Trooper Brown speculated as he wiped away a layer of dirt covering the glazed coating of C.R.A.P.'s metallic body. "Well anyway, meet C.R.A.P. my friends – this is the little guy who'll be piloting for us on our next mission," he announced to the Bigadons who stared at the robot confusedly. C.R.A.P. spouted a little fountain of oil onto the floor. "Woops – better fix that," Trooper Brown apologised as he ran a cloth over the robot and mopped up the mess. He set C.R.A.P. down, who shuffled out of view, off to attend to other duties around the ship, an oil leek trailing by his side.

"Tell me – what were you doing down in that temple all alone?" Calron asked when he thought he saw something glint inside the backpack Crede was handling.

"I'm sorry – we're not allowed to tell anyone except the council and the governor of events concerning the welfare of our people," Starna answered professionally, knowing the question was to arise sooner or later.

"Alright, alright, we respect that," Calron said as he paced the length of the passenger compartment. "Would we get a similar reply from the council if we were to ask them?"

"I'm not sure – perhaps it would be worthwhile should you try."

"Ok, on a further note, I will. Adaman, update mission status. It's our policy that we drop any passengers off before we take onboard any more. So, after these three are safe, we'll make another rescue at dawn."

"Then that should be four Bigadons back at home." This remark made something inside Starna click into place. She felt that it would be her fault if whoever was in danger died because help was elsewhere, bringing *her* home.

"No!" she pleaded. "We must go now – it could be too late by dawn!" Calron looked at her with genuine concern.

"We can't risk you three," he said in defence. "The next

rescue has been classified as high risk. That means there's more chance we'll be blown out of the sky than have any success."

"Then that will have to be that – we can't leave another of our kind suffering while we take comfort at his or her expense. Can you tell me the name of the person at risk?"

Calron thought for a moment before deciding that it wasn't necessary to withhold the information from her. He leaned over the command console and busied himself for a few seconds before pulling away, deep in thought.

"Anta Margul," he said after a short delay.

"Please," she continued, "We must go now."

There was a moment's pause as Calron rubbed his head; all eyes were on him,

"Alright," Calron agreed. "But only as long as your company are up for it."

Starna looked at them hopefully. Crede nodded and Heme pretended to be unaware of the situation.

"We… agree, don't we Heme?" The bewildered Bigadon gave a subtle gesture of approval. She was annoyed that she had to rope her companions into it, but she knew that neither could bear the guilt if the distressed caller was found dead because of their delay – ultimately, they agreed with her.

"OK then - C.R.A.P., follow through with mission objectives."

"Mission objectives have been recognised – initiation procedure in process," C.R.A.P. responded automatically. He waddled along to the command deck and uploaded his mainframe to divert the ship on a new course. "Estimated time until arrival – 15 minutes at full ion thrust."

"Looks like we won't be waiting long," Trooper Brown said thankfully and removed his helmet. Although his face could be seen through his visor, it gained a whole new degree of clarity without it – in truth, his helmet did not do his features justice and clouded them enough that his image became vague.

Starna was pleased to see that he was neither shockingly attractive nor off-putting, though he did have a certain rough appeal which went in his favour. He set his rounded helmet at his side and began to sip contentedly. The chilled contents produced condensation on his cup.

Both Tank, the metal giant, and Slayer, the more streamlined robot, disappeared momentarily to prepare their weaponry for the task ahead.

Starna was speechless at the independence of the two warriors, who were both just a pair of circuit boards wired up to metallic components. But she found it both amazing and disturbing that they could prepare for the future without the need of a living brain to guide them.

"Impressive, aren't they?" Trooper Brown said behind a distant smile. He had obviously noticed her staring at their mechanical counterparts. "They're some of the latest on the market. They've been helping us for years, and because there have been no major advances in technology since they were presented to us, Coda has allowed us to keep them."

"Yes, there is something quite special about them," Crede said, also with an interest in the robots. "I trust that they are very efficient on the battlefield."

Starna looked at him knowingly. "Yes Crede – I can tell you that – I had to confront one while you and Heme were shaking underneath our supply pile." At that moment she had created something of a spark in the air and the Alpha Team burst into laughter, a reaction that none of the Bigadons expected.

"I-I – I," Heme flustered defensively, "I was unarmed and couldn't do anything to protect myself," he protested, finding no humour in them mocking his actions.

The next ten minutes passed with both races keeping the

dialogue in a friendly and respectful context with each other. The Bigadons had all been relieved that the humans were willing to stop asking probing questions of the operation they were carrying out before they had been rescued. Calron had taken interest in the treasure they had found, but Starna knew that he would consider it nothing more than a large diamond, not the solitary hope that an entire civilisation was reliant upon.

When the countdown timer at the command console buzzed and then flashed red, the Alpha Team departed from the company of the Bigadons, leaving them with a single piece of advice – stay where they were.

When Starna repeated this order to her companions for the third time, Crede double-checked that the stone was securely in place in the bag he carried it in, and Heme gripped the knotted mess that bound him to the bench and said,

"I'm not sure I could get out even if I wanted to, anyway, Starna." When C.R.A.P. verified that the first stages of the operation were beginning, Heme and Crede began discussing the probable course of action that the humans were likely to take.

"They won't have to leave the ship if they're doing what I think they're doing," Crede said as he secured a loose belt that hung near his waist.

"Traction beams are prepared," C.R.A.P.'s monotonous voice echoed.

"And what, exactly, is that?" Heme asked his close friend.

"C.R.A.P. just confirmed that traction beams are going to be used," he said, aware of the robot's updates in the background. "Traction beams have even been put into some of our vessels lately – they can suspend an object in the air for as long as they are operational, giving a similar effect to that of a field of magnetism. So, if they can grab the target with a traction beam, pull it out of the area and then bring it onto the ship, they probably won't even need to leave the comfort of this aircraft themselves, unless, of course, they miss their target." Starna was pleased to see that they were making conversation just as willingly as they would have done in any other situation, despite their raised anxiety levels.

"There's little chance of that with today's technology," Starna reassured them. The Alpha Team, including the metal giant, Tank, and the smaller model, Slayer, rallied at the command deck. Adaman, Calron and Trooper Brown took their designated seats beside the consoles on the deck and began the tasks they each had to carry out in conjunction with one another.

"Two kilometres and closing," C.R.A.P. informed them. "Estimated time to arrival at objective 20 seconds and counting. Decreasing velocity and altitude to meet with objective at pre-set speed. Ship readjusting module in progress – air velocity increasing by estimated 45%. Traction beams locked and operational in five…"

The Bigadons could hear the exterior of the ship adjusting to gain more air resistance, slowing its rapid advance towards the target. Trooper Brown, Adaman and Calron began the exchange of orders.

"Don't worry back there – everything's fine," Trooper Brown confirmed, whilst quickly interacting with touch-sensitive screens and readjusting levers. All three human members of the Alpha Team worked well together, and Starna was sure they were not only doing this for show – she had the feeling that they had got used to the frantic pace of work they had suddenly adopted many times before.

"Heat-masking is operational," Trooper Brown told Adaman who worked with an assortment of dials on his console, responding to the changing status.

"Traction beams have located objective and are now

operational. Target is secured," C.R.A.P. said in his usual toneless voice.

Suddenly the sound of gunfire racked the conjoined compartments – it disrupted the exchange of orders and unsettled the passengers. The Gatheren responsive assault on their craft was nothing short of vicious – even when they could see that the ship had not come to attack them.

Luckily, not many of the shots hit their mark due to the heat-masking and lock-protective fields surrounding the craft. Unfortunately a stray shot struck one of the engines but the reserve would provide enough power for them to continue their journey. When C.R.A.P. informed them that the target had withdrawn a safe distance from the stationary Gatheren forces, Calron declared it safe to open the passenger deck so the target could be loaded on board.

Gusts of air blasted inside the deck when the compartment opened, but the Bigadons had assured their safety among many belts and straps.

The battered form of a Bigadon soldier was lifted up, the traction beams directing the fragile body so it met with Adaman who was ready with a stretcher. Trooper Brown then rushed the wounded soldier into the command deck where both Calron and C.R.A.P. were engaged in creating as great a distance as possible between the ship and the Gatheren ground forces it had just passed over seconds before. Adaman slammed the lever to shut the hatch, but to both his dismay and annoyance it refused to obey and jammed, remaining half-open.

Furthering their misery, the arrival of two Gatheren howler air units spelled extreme danger for the passengers on the ship. The transparent shiny exterior of the two craft allowed them to see the armoured heads of the pilot Reptans, cackling insanely as they charged their weapons to fire at the escaping Alpha Team aircraft.

It was then that Adaman reacted, a mental mustering of fear and hatred preparing his body for the unleashing of a mysterious potent force, in the form of Karma. Lightning arced from his fingertips, conducted on the alien materials of the pursuing air units and caused them to capsize. They veered into each other's sides and jittered, set alight by the mystical force Adaman had summoned to the aid of his allies. The two units made an uncontrolled rapid descent into the sea below, their vessels disappearing into the brackish depths. Explosions created fountains many feet high, signifying their demise.

Tank then intervened, lumbering forward like a wall, and used both arms to drag the hatch to a close. The vibes Adaman's magical output had created electrified the air, the hot intensity of the lightning making the compartment strangely humid for a moment.

He collapsed onto the bench opposite the three awe-struck Bigadons, who stared at him in both admiration and confusion. Although Starna had strong suspicions of this person being similar in description to the famed *wizards*, or *karmiacs* as they were more commonly known, she had not truly suspected that he possessed these powers which she thought were merely myth.

But he had demonstrated his potential to them all, and when asked about the experience, answered, "It is as if every nerve in your body is set ablaze." He remained silent for a good while afterwards.

After their close escape, thanks to the spectacle Adaman had created, the journey to the Plaza went faster than Starna would have expected. Five minutes before arrival she was allowed into the command deck where the multi-purpose android Slayer leaned over the battered form of Anta, various surgical tools protruding from an area on his chest, drawing precise lines where the creature needed attention. As the alien's anatomy was very similar to that of a human, the procedure was left relatively unchanged and proved to be a success, although the Bigadon was still in a near-death state after the robot had finished operating. Slayer predicted that chances of this creature surviving were minimal.

Starna looked over the cut and bruised face of this courageous spy, who despite offering his life in service of his people, had been rewarded with little more than critical or permanent damage to some areas of his body, or even worse - death.

She found it hard to brace the tears that gathered when she saw how laboured each breath had become, how difficult it was for him to continue living. She immediately recognised his pain as the work of the Gatheren, the sick nature of their culture and their determination to eradicate the kinder kin.

Slayer ejected antiseptic sprays on the areas where infection was liable to spread. Just as C.R.A.P. had done, he archived the creature's physical and behavioural data and moved away from the stretcher, in the knowledge that he had done his work to the level that was expected of him.

Touch-down outside the Plaza walls was made slower and more controlled, mainly because there was a passenger onboard in a grave condition.

The humans bode the Bigadons farewell, requesting that they enquire of the council on matters later – their main priority was to ensure that Anta was given back into the hands of his people in the best condition possible, in spite of everything that had happened to him. When he had been securely loaded onto a stretcher he was carried into the Plaza, where the two races then bode each other a fond farewell; they were to meet again. With that they disappeared behind the mighty walls and Anta was sent home again with warm wishes for recovery, even from those who didn't know him or fully comprehend the terrible ordeal he had endured.

Chapter XXI
GEMINI

Anya sat quietly as the armoured transport truck rolled over the icy tundra. She, like the many other gifted children that accompanied her, had been taken from the human settlements in the Far East to their new home – a massive fortified structure called GEMINI. The structure was supposedly only one quarter smaller in height than the mighty Bigadon Plaza walls – an astounding achievement when the full scale of their neighbouring races' central population hub was taken into consideration.

GEMINI boasted teaching facilities, military training protocol programs, and houses inside the actual structure itself, like a whole city living within an iron shell. Here Anya would spend her years until she became an adult and was granted permission to leave. It had been explained to her many times that this would only be possible if she were to reach the standards expected of her; as did the hundreds of other frightened and secluded children, twenty of whom accompanied her on this journey. They were all thirteen years old, as far as she knew, and they were all to be placed in the same class.

They were the first group to be brought to GEMINI. The others were to follow shortly.

The children shook uncomfortably as the vehicle rumbled when it reached the uneven grounds a kilometre from their destination. As the truck cleared the icy hills, Anya thought about her parents – they would miss her, and she would miss them desperately too. They understood that it was too risky to keep her living with them in their vulnerable home settlement though, and had tried feebly to disguise the fact that the Gatheren were nearing them and they were in danger of being attacked. And, even though she was moving to a place where she would be safe, her parents were still unguarded in their home town. Every waking hour she found herself praying for their well-being. They were tough though, and she had confidence in them and their ability to survive.

"We're here," Colonel Draig announced from the front passenger seat. The vehicle came to a stop, and two armed guards hauled the truck doors open.

A freezing wind howled inside, and the children were briskly marched out and up a winding path, from which they could see the true majesty of GEMINI, the greatest accomplishment of the humans on Pharsee.

It stood high into the sky, its armoured bulk making it appear like a huge slab of metal. At first, Anya didn't believe that any structure could be ready in time for their arrival, a date they had received years before, to house a city complex, but she was quickly corrected as they moved under GEMINI's all-consuming shadow. She could remember the 'traditional' letter in the post they had received, the arguments her parents had – all coming back to her as she saw what all the fuss had been about.

"I heard this place is nuclear proof," she heard one child say close behind her as he trudged through the knee-high snow.

"Why do you think they would go to all this trouble for us?" another asked.

Colonel Draig marched beside them, his uniform snow-speckled and darkened by the dampness. He had pale white skin, and occasionally shades of purple and red would cross his face when he became angry.

"You're here because we need to protect you. We cannot afford to lose our children, because you are our next generation empowered to retain human control over areas of this planet," he answered stoutly. The children behind Anya went silent.

The Colonel, escorted by two uniformed and clean-shaven guards, approached the massive entrance into GEMINI, which, when opened, was like the gaping mouth of a giant. No doubt military craft and ground forces were on regular patrol in and out of the city complex, which made ease of access a necessity.

The children tailed the Colonel and his two escorts through a winding labyrinth of armoured corridors until they were brought into the structure's interior – indeed, inside was a small city, but a city like none Anya had seen before. Although GEMINI was currently desolate, the air of achievement swept around them on entry – this was the place in which Pharsee's finest of the next generation were soon to occupy. Shops, schools, bunkers, sports facilities, restaurants and cinemas were all present, each possessing splendour uncommon to regular public buildings –they looked like they had been made for royalty.

Stunned mutterings sounded behind her. The children were impressed, and she couldn't blame them, but perhaps the insides of the buildings would be less spectacular.

Again, she was quickly proven wrong as the Colonel directed them to a large briefing room on the outskirts of the central city complex.

Inside, the children passed through a network of decorated corridors until they were seated in a wide, open hall with a podium at the far end. The whole place looked so formal to her – it had none of the inviting sense that her home with her parents had.

More guards were on duty inside what Anya had begun

to think of as a Town Hall of sorts. Their armaments were sleek and deadly, and she wondered whether they were really prepared to meet a crisis, or if they were just standing there single-mindedly for show.

"Children," Colonel Draig's sharp voice broke the hushed silence. "Welcome to your new home. Shortly, you will each be assigned to a flat room which you will share with three others when more pupils arrive. These rooms will be chosen at random, and over the first two years of your being here there will be several changes in the housing plans; your house mates will be reshuffled in order to allow you to meet new people, and at the end of these two years you will choose who will be your flatmates permanently."

A ghostly silence fell over the children; from what Anya could tell, many of them didn't like the idea of being placed to and fro. She knew that perhaps several would already know who they wanted to stay with. She just prayed that at the end of the day she would be left with people she liked.

Already she could see how different this place was from her school in her home town. The children here were gifted, and this was a place where they could perfect their abilities, no doubt without the hindrance of the handfuls of rebels she could remember from her old school who wanted to do their own thing. Here, she knew no such rebellion would be possible – the Colonel had told them that a strict discipline regime had been undertaken to keep the children in line.

"Timetables will be handed out shortly. You will spend four days of the week attending normal classes. On the fifth day, you may choose in which areas you wish to study. The weekend is yours, though remember that to do well here you need to put in the work, so revising lessons gone over in class is advisable. My colleague, Miss Pince, will take you from here. Any problems may be reported to her whenever she is available. We will all try to be responsible for giving you the best education possible."

Anya opened her bag and pulled out the blackened form of a small bear, and clutched it tight to her chest for comfort. She didn't care how she looked in front of the other children - it comforted her in her time of need.

Miss Pince, a tall lean woman in her early twenties, raised herself from her chair and strolled over to where the children sat. Her blonde hair was tied up in a tight bun, and she wore smart clothes that shone under the bright overhead lights of the hall. Her fingernails were immaculate and she obviously had no financial worries.

"Hello, children," she said in a sickly-sweet note. "Our first lesson of the day is swimming. You've all been granted trunks and swimsuits to fit you, and so we'll make use of the available equipment while the other departments are made ready for you. So, it's off to the pool we go," she said a little too enthusiastically, though the children seemed encouraged to have a high-spirited teacher accompany them- far better than the sharp and demanding restrictions the Colonel had implied on his initial meeting with the children.

A stream of kids edged passed her, but Anya was adamant not to be left out. She held her teddy bear tight and walked at her own pace out of the hall and along with the children ahead of her.

Miss Pince cocked her head as they left the Town Hall and called to her and the other children trailing behind.

"Come on now, don't be shy! The water will be warm, and I'm sure that's some consolation to the non-swimmers among you after your journey through the freezing tundra."

Anya forced herself to hurry and caught up with the main group of kids a short run ahead.

One girl, with short, swept-up curly hair withdrew from the

group to speak to her. She had some features similar to Anya's own. Her hair was neat and tidy, and they both had brown eyes. That's where the similarities ended.

"What are you doing carrying that mucky thing around with you?" she asked spitefully, looking disdainfully at Anya's bear. She prodded it and then screwed up her face. Anya pulled her fluffy friend out of her reach.

She silently skipped ahead of her. *Great,* she thought. *An enemy already* –now she felt was the time to look for a few friends to even the score.

"This way, children." Miss Pince pointed further into the city complex of GEMINI, to a small yellow building smelling heavily of chlorine. Anya noted that this place was the swimming pool.

In her haste to draw into the crowd of children amassing outside the yellow building, a few feet before where Miss Pince stood rigidly, she trod on the heels of someone she felt she had known before. It became clear to her then, as the girl turned to face her that this was one of her best friends she had known during nursery and early primary school – Joy.

Anya found herself lost for words.

"Joy!" was all she could muster, and the two gripped each other tight and laughed, relieved and happy at their reunion.

"Anya! I never thought I would ever see you again. I was starting to worry that there'd be nobody here I'd get on with – now I've found you I'm no longer alone!" She was startled at how mature Joy looked already – for a girl of thirteen, she appeared several years older.

Anya laughed with her, because she knew that was how she felt too when she saw her. She quickly stashed her teddy bear in her bag; she wasn't likely to need him again for a while, now that she had found an old friend.

Miss Pince cleared her throat in an attention-seeking

manner. Anya soon began to find her silky-smooth tone of voice irritating.

"Children – enter in single file. You each have a locker and cubicle under the same number given to you on entry."

The children slowly shuffled inwards, and Anya found herself third in the queue, with Joy just behind.

They passed into a large corridor with two conjoined changing rooms. On the wall beside them was a list of names, with a number opposite. Anya scanned down the list.

Anya Lowing   No. 56

Quickly memorising the number, she moved through the half open door into the changing rooms.

They were enormous. Hundreds of cubicles, about the size of the bathroom she had at home, were stacked together in neat rows, with the lockers occupying the entire length of the right side. The changing room was cream in colour, and warm with the air of the swimming pool finding its way through the doors whenever they were opened. She trailed her bag at her feet and jogged down the cubicle numbers. She was out of breath by the time she reached fifty-six.

Inside the cubicle were a sink, a toilet and a bench to set her stuff on while she got changed. She found her locker code tagged to the cubicle wall. They had all been given swimsuits to suit their size, and for a moment Anya was tempted to set hers aside and put on the one her parents had bought for her. *No,* she thought, *that might make me look disrespectful.*

She patiently waited for Joy to accompany her out of the changing rooms. Joy hopped out of her cubicle, fighting with her clothes as they threatened to drop from the loose bundle she had made them into. The two of them moved to the giant lockers on the right, and watched the expressions on the faces of the other groups of girls who rushed passed them, lost and bewildered as to where everything went.

She spotted her number, fifty-six, faster than she thought possible. It was four columns above ground level, and she stretched up, but it was beyond arms reach. There was no way she could get at it. Joy seemed to be having the same problem.

"How are we expected to get to them?" her friend said as she swept back her custard-blonde hair. "Oh, wait, look," she added and pointed to a roll-along stepladder, tucked away in the corner. "We could use that." Anya rushed to help her pull along the ladder, which was connected to a short railing. Joy stepped up and twisted the dial on the locker, and it popped open. She was happy to see how much space she had; her clothes were easily stowed away in it.

The banging of locker doors echoed throughout the room. Anya followed her example, using the stepladder to gain height and quickly stuffing her clothes and her bag into her locker. She had difficulty getting it shut, and Joy giggled mildly in the background as she played with the dial, turning it at extreme angles in an attempt to get it to lock into place.

They pushed the stepladder back where they had found it, and together walked out of the changing rooms.

The swimming pool was the most stunning thing they had seen since their arrival, with the exception of the massive exterior of GEMINI. The deep-sea smells hung richly in the air; the swimming pool was built around the scene of a cliff-side spa – rocks were tucked into the four corners of the pool, and the curvatures that gave the area shape were adorned with swirling decoratative lights. The waves reflected onto the roof, which was a large painting of various sea tales told in recent centuries.

Joy pinched her swimsuit – they were comfortable, much more comfortable, Anya found, than the ones her parents had bought her, but she supposed this was because they were wanted to feel welcome. They gave out an iridescent sheen, and were made to look like the scales of a sea-dwelling entity, such as a mermaid.

Joy looked at Anya mischievously. Her face formed a deep grin that stretched up just below her high-set cheekbones. Anya knew what she had in mind. Before she even asked, Joy gripped her hand and raced towards the edge of the pool. They both went under with a loud splash, sending a shot of warm air upwards, shattering the glass-like layer of the surface.

They emerged in a fit of laughter, just as Miss Pince strolled out of the staff changing rooms. She wore her usual smart business suit, but they noticed a new item on her clothing - a delicate area of intricate embroidery, which spelled, *Fiona Pince*.

"I hadn't given instructions for anyone to enter the pool yet," she snapped suddenly, her usually casual voice disappearing.

"We're sorry miss," Joy apologised behind a wide grin, gripping Anya's hand as they both left the warmth of the pool, the air around it suddenly seeming much cooler.

"I don't know what you're playing at, but I don't find anything amusing at you two making a spectacle of yourselves," she said as she looked at them over the top of her designer glasses.

The other children had gathered at the edge of the pool; Anya surveyed them all, knowing that there would only be this handful for a few more days at the most, before GEMINI became swarmed by talented children.

Not all of them seemed as gifted as they were made out to be, she thought. For instance, Pamela, the girl she recognised as the one who had approached her on their way to the pool. There wasn't anything that had appeared immediately recognisable as 'talent' in that one; unless attitude issues counted.

"Today, we will give you some leisure time – a free swim for everyone here," Miss Pince began. *Is that it?* Anya thought.

"I thought you said we were getting lessons," one boy said,

to break an awkward silence. He blushed when she set her gaze upon him.

"Oh, but it is a lesson." The wavy light patterns from the pool jerked across her figure. "You will be given time to do as you please – within the regulations of course – and soon you will learn about the rarity of time to yourselves in here. We expect the best from you all. You are the next and only generation left to take over operations on this planet. You have to be ready, if we are to secure our existence here." She perked her head up high. "I have other duties I need to attend to. Be aware that you are under constant supervision, although you may not realise it. Hopefully we'll learn something of your character from our observations." She departed back into the changing rooms before ushering out a handful of girls who where dawdling inside. The children were left alone in the pool. Were they being watched? There were no obvious signs. Anya dismissed the idea and acted naturally, just as she would have had she been alone or with a group of friends. Today, she would test her boundaries.

Once again, Joy grabbed her hand and they jumped in together. The relaxing temperature of the water and the calming sea salts helped her unwind, as she had been like a coiled spring since the day she had been taken away from her parents. She was surprised, when she asked Joy, to find out that it had been a week since she had left her home; it seemed like so much longer.

"I know – I miss my parents too," Joy admitted as she swept a length of hair from her wet forehead. "It won't be so bad once we've had time to adjust." Anya didn't feel convinced.

Together they explored the length of the pool. Gushes of water spread over them as the other children dropped in like bombs. There was more than enough space to fit in ten times their number – like everything else they had seen on entry, it was huge.

Ornamental fountains adorned each side –engravings of great ocean-dwelling creatures were spread along the walls, with great emphasis being put on detail. Anya had never before seen anything which came so close to the quality of this place. She imagined the vast budget the people were given to create it. Under the water something hit her heel.

A boy, with dark hair, tanned skin and green eyes emerged quickly to apologise.

"Sorry – you'd think with all this space there'd be no chance of me hitting someone." Anya smiled warmly.

"No problem," she accepted his apology immediately. "What is your name? It's about time me and Joy," she said as she grabbed Joy's arm to get her attention, "got to know some people."

"I'm Albert," he answered, as he handled a ball he had found at the poolside.

"I'm Anya. Well, looks like I'll be seeing you around. We're off to search the pool – feel like coming?" Joy subtly kicked her leg under the water.

"Uh… sure," he answered hesitantly, and called on his friend Ronald to group up with them.

"What did you do that for?" Joy whispered to her Albert explained their invitation to his friend.

"Good manners, and face it Joy," – Anya stared around to emphasize her point; "we can't afford to be left alone in here, especially when the new groups arrive. The place will be swamped with children then – chances are we'll be separated."

"I won't let that happen," Joy declared stubbornly, but she knew she had little power to prevent it.

"We're ready now – you lead," Albert said as Ronald, a large, solidly-built child with a very youthful face, glided behind them.

Joy remained static.

"Go Joy," Anya urged her forward and in a group of four,

they swam further down the watery enclosure. Anya was proud that she had already met two others – and there was some male support, right when she needed it. The more the merrier, her father used to say.

They paddled until their legs became tired and they decided to stop for a short break.

"So, Albert, Ronald, tell me a bit about yourselves," Anya said, hoping to become acquainted with them. She watched as three children opposite them bombed into the pool in unison, sending ripples through the unsettled water.

"Well, I'm…" he began, not sure where to start.

"I'm sorry," Joy interrupted. "I can't understand you when you mutter like that."

Anya splashed Joy in the face, and watched as she struggled to stay aloft in the water. Their new company laughed.

"Don't mind Joy, she's just shy," Anya apologised on her behalf.

"I am not!" Joy shouted, when Miss Pince appeared on the scene again, blowing loudly into a whistle to get the children's attention.

She signalled for the children to gather close so they could hear her clearly. It took several minutes until she had rallied them all up.

"Swim's over, I'm afraid. I'll meet you all outside the changing rooms. Don't be long." With that, she retraced the way she had come in and left them to it. Joy sighed, reluctant to leave the warmth of the pool.

"Wonder where we're going now," Anya heard Albert say as he climbed onto the poolside soaking wet. Anya and Joy hurried into the changing rooms – there would be no hanging around if they were to get out in decent time. They swept their ringing-wet hair out of their eyes and moved purposefully away from the warm air.

Chapter XXII
The Lost Metropolis

Starna carried the wounded Anta to the nearest medical silo and departed with the knowledge that he was in safe hands. Heme and Crede walked by her side, and after a long period on foot, with several breaks to rest their aching feet in between, they reached the council tower. A feeling of familiarity accompanied them as they gazed upon the sacred building.

The structure was large and adorned with different symbols of religion – it depicted Bigadon society and gave them an example of achievement which they were encouraged to follow. It was the primary beacon planet-wide for the Bigadons, and only matters of extreme importance were ever brought to the council's attention at a time of war. But undoubtedly Starna knew that they would be delighted by her find, and perhaps could find some use for the artefact she had obtained on her expedition.

She began to stride up the massive staircase which coiled around the building like a snake. Heme and Crede followed behind her, excited by the idea of telling about their adventurous journey to their friends and family. Starna's mind was divided between two things – meeting with the council which would happen shortly, and finding Ark, her uncle whom she loved dearly, and her only close relative in the Plaza.

At the top of the staircase a guard stood under a small plate of roofing from where he was shielded from the rays of Rako, the huge sun. It was unfortunate that the Bigadons had had to establish their main population hub in a warm climate which they were not accustomed to, but it was necessary to depart from their home sector in the icy north when the Gatheren attacked and obliterated many of their settlements.

It had become commonplace, and even fashionable in some cases, for a Bigadon to shave its face, arms and back so as to not trap the heat that smothered the Plaza every morning at dawn. This was the case with the guard that blocked the entrance to the council quarters, even though he spent all day under the tiles that had been provided for his own comfort. Such was the measures the Bigadons were willing to take to escape from the tyranny of the Gatheren – climate adaptation being the least of their worries while many other more serious problems were present.

"We request entry," Starna said in the hope that she would have to spend no more time under the glaring sun to introduce herself, Heme and Crede, who both seemed eager to move into the shade.

"Ahh – Starna? Is that you?" the guard asked in a gruff voice, peering into the strong sunlight where the three recent explorers faced him.

"Yes, and these were my companions for the expedition – may we enter?"

"Of course," the guard replied and shuffled aside – he gave them the impression that they could have walked over him if they were not permitted entry, as it was well known that the heat sapped energy – something that a guard of the council needed much of, despite remaining stationary for most of their shifts. This had not been the case in the icy north, where they could happily remain dutiful and energised for hours at a time. The new conditions they encountered when the council had been evacuated from the had left their profession questionable in its worth; it took little time for the sun to leave them weak.

When they entered the breathtaking interior of the tower the heat was quickly drawn from them. It appeared much larger on the inside than it did from the outside, and as they paced through the building this impression only grew stronger.

After five minutes of wandering in search of the council they finally heard chatter, a stream of different voices spoken in edgy tones.

Heme and Crede recognised these voices as those of the council – a miscellaneous bunch, but they were no doubt intellectuals, despite their appearance. The three visitors entered their chamber.

They had walked in during the middle of a heated debate, and a static vibe of anger and disapproval evoked a feeling of fright from them upon making their entrance.

"If you weren't so discreet about everything then you wouldn't have to hide behind a curtain of lies!" A small female figure, no higher than Starna's chest, shouted across the room, oblivious to their arrival.

"What are you talking about Shella? Honestly," a tall male replied with a feigned note of sarcasm, aware of the presence of guests.

"I'm talking about our metropolis in the west and Gazra!" she screamed, trying her hardest to put him back into line, although not picking up on the hint he was giving her. The name made the trio prick up their ears, their minds racing. Starna could remember it from somewhere, but a frustrating moment had arisen when she couldn't pinpoint when or where exactly.

Heme gasped behind her, for once coming up with something of use.

"Our next governor!" he exclaimed, drawing the eyes of the council, the small female councillor open-mouthed and muttering in shock.

"Oh we have visitors!" One male figure announced in an inviting voice, though it was apparent to all there that the visitors couldn't have chosen a worse time to drop in.

"What has happened to Gazra?" Crede asked, the image of the Chancellor-in-waiting on his mind. The question had been directed at the small council member whose mouth remained like a cave-opening until she found the composure to reply. She diverted her stare quizzically around the council ring in search of support, and finding none, started on an explanation herself.

"Well, you see – he – he got delayed from meeting with us here… and… can we help you?" she asked finally, her explanation not sufficient for either Heme or Crede. Starna silenced them with the knowledge that they would get nowhere questioning these people, *unless…*

"We're here because of this." Starna lifted the gem from out of Crede's backpack and did a slow arc at the front of the ring with it in her arms. Its gleaming exterior reflected the wondrous expressions on the faces of council.

"We and three other humans came a hair's-breadth from death for this."

"There were humans involved?" a voice asked from the ring, triggering a wave of disapproving mutterings throughout.

"Yes – but without their involvement we would be dead by now. Perhaps it is in your best interests to give them more credit," Starna replied defensively, finding a hidden part of herself that respected their neighbouring race more than she would have liked.

"They're only following the book, Starna," Crede whispered in her ear. "Remember – involvement from other races on a private mission is bad – the keyword being *private.*"

Starna wanted to, but restrained from, striking him.

"We appreciate the fact that you respect the humans," the council ringleader, a tall spindly character, said as he caressed the delicate fabrics of his robes. "But their involvement in this project was unwanted. Yet I suppose we can only thank them for bringing you to us safely," he admitted reluctantly. "May I see the Object?" he asked, outstretching his arms in a longing gesture.

"Of course." Starna took it upon herself to give him the stone personally. She approached the ring and offered it into his hands; her timing was perfect and she withdrew it as his fingers caressed its facets, plucking it back from under his eyes. The ring-leader was horrified at this action, his eyes narrowing in outrage, as he primed his voice box to shout at her.

"No!" Starna shocked him into submission, her actions so alien to the council who had never experienced anything other than complete and immediate obedience from any lower class citizen.

"I know there's something going on here that you're not letting us in on," she said as she stared out each of the council members in turn. "Tell me of this metropolis. Tell me of Gazra, and what has become of him. I risked my life for this thing, as did my companions, and for this I think we deserve to know." Heme and Crede were also stunned by her actions, and though they silently withdrew a few steps, she knew they would back her up.

The ring-leader merely laughed, his face becoming a portrait of bemusement.

"What are you doing, infiltrator? I wish not to be involved in your little games," he demanded.

"All I want in return for this 'priceless' artefact is answers. It's really quite simple – I know that I won't get them from you by fair-play – as do you. I'm not a trained negotiator, but I know what I need to do to get some answers."

"I suggest you give the stone to me now before I call on the guards." Starna scanned the length of the room, and once she found a suitable exit – a window leading down to a balcony below - her confidence was restored.

"Call them," she dared, her voice almost breaking in an effort to steady her nerves, but she quickly conquered them. "I'll be long gone with this treasure before they even arrive."

The ring-leader looked at the open window and then met her eyes again. He swallowed his anger.

"I see. Well perhaps it is best that you sit down," he said, gesturing to the single empty chair remaining in the council circle.

Reluctantly, she obeyed his request, yet she could not fully settle herself under the gaze of their mistrusting eyes.

She listened attentively as he dropped his head in sorrow and began to tell her of the metropolis in the west.

"I'm not sure –" the small female figure began, a worried expression crossing her troubled face.

"They are right – we will have to tell the public sometime Shella. It's better that we face our troubles in unity rather than in isolation. 'Strength in numbers'," he quoted distractedly. The female councillor tried to speak again, but the words never left her mouth. The other council members remained silent and observant, like a group of engrossed spectators.

"We had begun operations to move our people from the north down to the west, in a buried Pharseean city, where we previously uncovered this item." He lifted an arcane staff, which was commonly known to reside by him – it too, had become a symbol across entire planets of the importance of uncovering more artefacts from ancient Pharseean structures. The weapon was known to possess potentially destructive powers, functioning by methods the Bigadons simply did not understand. It had been handed down through generations, always finding its place beside the chair of the council ring leader.

"A Pharseean metropolis?" Heme asked in amazement, already thinking of the opportunity for further discovery and deeper insight into the culture of their ancestors.

"Yes. There were many items of value uncovered, and it seemed that we had come the closest ever to finding the treasures of our ancestors – one of them being the gem you hold in your hands. After the Gatheren attacked on our cities, we were forced to find a new place for our people to reside, and quickly. We moved them into the metropolis, and re-sealed it underground to hide them from the Gatheren who were stalking them. Communications were lost within three days. We have no further information, but we don't believe there is any way the pursuing enemy forces could have found them."

Starna found herself speechless, the disturbing knowledge of an isolated population forcing her to delve deeper.

"And that was it?" she asked. "Nothing more – they were just cut off altogether?"

"One transmission. That was all."

"Can I see this transmission?" she asked, hoping she wasn't pushing the boundaries too far. The council-ring eyed her suspiciously, as if even querying further into the topic was evil or perverse.

"*Now,* that is restricted information, and you cannot bargain yourself any further," he warned her, a hint of regret already tainting his voice as a result of having told her of the metropolis. "We respect your work on behalf of our people, and in time you will all be rewarded accordingly. Tell no-one of this, or we shall exile you from this place forever."

Pleased with the information she had drawn out of them, she passed the gem into the hands of the ring leader and exited, knowing that she would probably never hold an item of such value in her life again.

Heme and Crede both seemed just as startled when they left by her side as they had been on entry, and the council sharply dismissed them, as the closing of the chamber doors brought their meeting to an end.

• • •

After departing with Heme and Crede, who she scheduled to meet with the next day, Starna sought to find her uncle amongst the huge city-complex. The Plaza had always been a hard place to find anyone in, and she had often gotten lost when she and her uncle had moved there during her adolescence. On arrival, she had wandered around aimlessly, enjoying the bustle and the ever-changing populace when her uncle had gone off to find employment.

When she was sure she was on the right track, she followed it until the large bungalow her uncle had earned through his years of service came into sight. Patiently, she knocked on the door and waited.

Her uncle pulled it open and stood in front of her, his face ecstatic at the sight of her well-being.

"Starna! How are you? What happened? Did everything go ok?" She laughed as he picked her up and twirled her around, making their reunion public.

"Oh please, come in, come in!" He hurried her into the kitchen and she was surprised to see that he had done extensive work in making his place more suitable to her, specifically a room he had personally done up in preparation for her return.

"You went to all this trouble when I was away?" she asked, bewildered.

"Of course! I found myself very lonely all of a sudden, you know with all my middle-aged pals off to fight in the war, or creating weapons and so forth. So, I decided that I would make use of my spare time to make this place more welcoming for you."

"Well I have to say I'm impressed." She looked into the grey eyes of her uncle, and decided that she should share her knowledge with him, no matter what the consequences would be. She recalled the council's words, knowing that she could not withhold the information she had drawn out of them, especially in the company of her beloved uncle.

"Uncle, I want to tell you something." Ark met the eyes of his niece.

"You know you can tell me anything, Starna." She had confided many of her feelings, opinions and beliefs to him during their years in each other's company.

"I found a sacred treasure in the temple," she said, making things uncomplicated deliberately.

Ark stared blankly at her for a moment, and then jittered into response.

"What? You found one inscribed in legend?"

"Yes – it was like a diamond, and a huge one at that. It was hidden deep within the temple, and with the help of the humans we were able to get it to the council," she confessed.

"Humans went with you? What – why?" he asked confusedly, itching his greying hair that had thinned considerably over the years.

"We'd better sit down," she advised as she pulled a stool to her knees and did the same for her uncle. "The humans saved us as we were attacked – our ships were destroyed, we were stranded. We broadcast a signal for help and they were the first to respond. When they arrived, we – these things they... descended from the roof of the temple, like jellyfish, only larger and more vicious," she explained when she recalled the horrifying advance of their tentacles, tasting their targets before they fired masses of acid at their prey.

"Starna – what are you saying? Did you meet with our ancestors?" He placed a large hand on her shoulder and leaned forward to comfort her.

"I doubt it, but if they were our ancestors we truly have no hope any more. They ravaged the temple, blocked the exit and attacked both of us as well as the humans."

"Did Heme and Crede escape alright?"

"They're fine, they're fine," she said, relieved to have one piece of good news to share with him. "But when we escaped, I persuaded our human rescuers to pick up another of our kin." Ark chuckled suddenly.

"Do they do a 'twenty-four hour' service or something?" he grinned, recalling the strange phrases the humans used in advertising.

"When we arrived back here, I thought everything would have been OK," she continued. "But when we reached the council, we found them arguing. We questioned this, because it seemed serious. At first they tried to cover it up, dismissing their quarrels as a minor disagreement. Uncle – they mentioned Gazra, and I think something bad has come of him."

"But he's the heir to our entire civilisation! Without him we have no one! Are you sure you didn't mishear them?" he asked.

"I'm sure – they mentioned him by name. When we asked them of him, they brushed over it."

"Don't worry Starna, I'm sure everything will be fine."

"They wouldn't leave us in the dark, would they, uncle?"

"I'm sure they wouldn't," he replied uncertainly, now much more aware of the council's increasing separation from the public.

"And they mentioned a metropolis, a city they housed our people in to escape the Gatheren. It was another of the Pharseean structures. They said they had ordered to have it sealed over to prevent the populace being found. Contact was lost in three days." Ark felt disorientated for a moment, the rush of secret information he was hearing all of a sudden making everything more complicated.

"How did you find all this out?" he asked quietly, as if he no longer had the energy to speak normally.

"Negotiations, uncle." Ark smiled at her lovingly.

"My little negotiator," he said, his heart pounding rapidly at the thought of their people being left without a ruler – and worse, extinction, if the Gatheren were allowed to succeed in their bloody conquest…

● ● ●

His hands closed on hers, and his voice became a quiet, but stern whisper.

"This isn't just any old mission, Starna, this one could possibly bring the balance in this war to tip in our favour." She stared at him inquisitively, but there was no change in his expression. Perhaps her informer actually meant what he said this time – or been told to say, as it was from the holy tower of the council that he had been sent with this request. She noted that it was not often that informers were sent to personally deliver military objectives.

"I'll look at it, Hareo," she offered and took the mission tag from him before boding him farewell and returning into the kitchen of her uncle's spacious bungalow.

"Who was that?" Ark asked, having heard the knock on the door.

"It was nobody uncle." She rushed inside the room he had decorated for her, and for a moment she was worried that she had been sprung. Although Ark was aware that she had chosen to carry out high-risk missions as a profession, she always worried that he would try to persuade her to reject them.

She collapsed into the nesting area she had been given, a corner of the room adorned with luxurious silks and padding where she would sleep at night.

Almost immediately she heard a knocking on the bedroom

door – how could she have believed for a minute that her uncle had suddenly lost touch? Deep down she knew she could not avoid him, and she scolded herself for thinking it so easy.

"Starna – you're not seriously considering going on another 'military prowl'?" a term he often used for high-risk operations. "You've just returned from what seemed to be a perilous adventure. Don't you think a part of you deserves some rest?" he asked thoughtfully as he opened the door and walked in. She had tucked herself up in her nesting alcove, finding the smooth materials comforting as she fingered the briefing tag, lost in her thoughts.

"Yes, it's all very well saying that, Ark, but the Gatheren will not give up. If we don't fight, and fight until we can fight no more, who will?"

Her uncle made a noise that suggested he was accepting her viewpoint, for the first time in many years.

"You know what I think. You've already done your service, and more, for our people. Maybe it is you who should be staying at home while others fight the enemy. At least spend tomorrow here for the Celebratory Dance." She decided that she would, but continued to defend her profession and the risks she felt she had to take.

"There are hundreds of us mercenaries, uncle. We are our only local military power, and as such, we are the only ones able enough to protect the others. If our armies from other planets decide to step in, them maybe I'll ease up, but until then…"

"I'm not going to come to blows with you over this, Starna, but just remember that I'll always be here for you, no matter what."

"I've got to do this, uncle."

"If that's how you feel, you know you have my full support."

"I know," she said as she got up and embraced him affectionately.

Chapter XXIII
To and Fro

Collapsing into the comfort of his chair, Calron let out a quiet sigh of relief. After about an hour and a half of receiving cargo supplies though the supply bridge, and reshuffling all of his clothing into neatly packed folds, he took this moment to collect his thoughts. This was the first time the HAF had suggested staying put to monitor activity on any planet. *But why here? Wasn't this a charted planet, albeit a fairly new one at that?* He just couldn't get his head around the idea of Bigadons perhaps being more secretive than he suspected. But he had learnt a valuable lesson from Adaman on this particular topic: trust no-one who has potentially dangerous secrets to hide.

Progress of the primary rescue mission had stalled due to a damaged engine as the result of a sustained alien attack. Engineers had informed him that the *Alpha One* would be grounded for a couple of days at the least, even with the aid of Tank's new found mechanical skills. Clearing his already over-crowded thoughts, he spun on his chair to face the monitor in front of him, and with the pressing of a panel, the screen came to life.

"Greetings candidate number 030006439-Calron Udan Lowing. Please choose the area which you would like to explore." The Alpha Team A.I. jittered into being, assuming the form of a small holographic nova the size of his hand, which hovered above the keypad he was working on. He liked the fact that A.I.s spoke to people directly and communicated with them personally.

Calron leaned backwards in his chair as a series of accessible options came onto the display screen. His immediate reaction was to smile; only this computer ever addressed him by his full name, which in a strange way gave the machine a sort of personality that appealed to him. Sitting up straight he briefly scanned all the available options until he found what he was looking for - Universal News.

To his dismay, the first news headline brought on screen was not related to human progress, achievement or any other form or event to cause celebration. It was of death and murder on the human planet Plato - another neighbouring solar body in the Conquest System...

CARGO ZEPPELIN
ATTACKED BY TERRORISTS
PLATO'S STATION SHOCKED

He felt as if a cold knife had been pushed deep into his chest. Frantically he continued to read, praying that it was not history repeating itself...

Lowing Commercial Business Zeppelin *Airborne* was utterly destroyed in what is believed to be a terrorist attack...chaos... no survivors found...

No...it can't be...again? He simply would not believe what he was reading, his mind trying in a futile effort to rearrange the tiny black pixels of the headline to change the story completely. Suddenly he lost himself in painful memories he thought he had shut away forever...

● ● ●

"Now Calron, I don't want you to be causing havoc with that wind-sail of yours. And make sure that you get home in time for 17.30 hours. Understand?" his mother ordered, her voice clear enough that Calron could detect the hint of 'I don't want a repeat of last time'.

His mother's eyes were large and pale blue in colour and they caught the artificial light projected from the many bulbs that were placed on the upper decks. Her features were attractive, with her pointy chin and slender nose. Her hair was jet black, held in place by a pearl cuff that interloped from the top of her fringe to the back of her neck. She had a reputation for being a very intimidating woman. Her perfume smelt strongly of roses that had just blossomed on a fresh summer's day, her working top navy blue in colour bearing oily stains from where she had been adjusting the engines in an attempt to make them more efficient.

"Yes, mother," he said, sighing, aware of what she was referring to.

Nearly three weeks ago Calron had been flying with his teenage friends Nara, Bobo and Jim, on their adored wind-sails. During a game of skyball he had attempted to impress them by sailing through the construction work of his new house, chasing the ball that soared away from him. The result was Calron's overconfidence bringing calamity – he caught the tip of his right wing on a recently welded girder, which snagged the edges of the fibre wire, tangling both him and his wind-sail up in a knotted mess. *Damnit.*

He was thankful, and extremely lucky, as the fibre wire acted as a safety net, preventing him from falling to his death. It took nearly two hours *after* his friends had returned with help to cut him loose, after they had switched off the electrical grid to prevent other potentially hazardous incidents. He had escaped the ordeal bearing only minor cuts and bruises, with the exception of a nasty scar that ran from his forehead down narrowly avoiding his left eye. He chuckled in the hospital bed alongside his pals later that day... could have been worse. Little did he know that fate was about to intervene.

Once again he arranged to meet his friends on the viewing dome of the zeppelin. Drawing forth the hatch he directed them through the interior of his floating home until they reached the open-topped landing dock where they had left their wind-sails. They started them up. Hovering now three meters above the landing dock they briefly arranged teams with Calron and Nara on one and Bobo and Jim on the other. With that sorted, Bobo quickly recapped on the rules of fair play and waited expectantly for some form of acknowledgement. Nods went all around as the pairs then quickly discussed team tactics which usually involved trickery, such as the exchange of meaningless whispers in an attempt to make the opposition feel uneasy. Some, however, did involve the odd strategy or two on how to best make use of the available space or surrounding scenery during the game. The rules were simple - get the ball in the opposition's half of the court and into the open box as soon as possible by any means necessary, as long as no violence was used or rules broken.

Unexpectedly Calron's father, Dante, strolled by, cradling their new-born baby daughter. His father was tall and quite muscular from the labour of having to keep his 'girl' in the sky. On occasion his wife teased him about whether or not he actually knew how to keep his zeppelin afloat, but he was good hearted and always replied with, 'I'll take that as a compliment, dear.'

His brown leather jacket and rugged boots were some of his most well known possessions, and his reason for wearing them so often (he had a wealth of other garments stashed away) was that they kept him warm on a cold day at work or at high altitudes. His hair was dark brown, almost black, and fine to the touch. His bright turquoise eyes shone like diamonds, even under the starry night sky as he paraded along his 'girl'.

The baby was silent. That made a pleasant change and the look on his father's face was both one of relief and astonishment. Calron swiftly glided over towards him on his wind-sail, adjusting the engine to optimal effect, so as not to awaken the new-born. His father looked curiously at him,

"Does it still work?"

Calron immediately double-checked the device on which he was leaning over.

"Good as new - thanks Dad," he replied gratefully.

His father nodded. After his crash he had helped him repair his wind-sail, and it wasn't the first time he had been given help by his father on the machine. Once or twice they had taken it apart in order to replace the over-used engine, to be refitted with a newer model.

"Well, let's see you in action," he insisted.

Calron grinned, and without hesitation about-turned and zoomed to his group. He repeatedly looked over towards where his father was sitting and was delighted to discover that his mother too, was now on the scene watching him in action.

"Ready Calron?" Nara asked.

"Sure!"

The game started and the ball launched into the air. Bobo was already on it and fired across to Jim who slammed it into the box. A beep indicated a fair point scored. The counter started again and once more it was launched. This time Nara had retrieved the ball, swiftly dodging Jim and passing it to Calron. Bobo blocked the box but, with a fake pass to Nara, his attention was momentarily diverted and, with a diving slam, Calron drove the ball into the specified scoring area. 'Beep!' Applauses from his mother and father could be heard alongside the wakened baby's laughter. After about fifteen minutes of passing and scoring the game was in full swing when suddenly the alarms blared out. His parents and baby sister disappeared into the command bridge to see what all the commotion was about. Abandoning the game of skyball, Calron and his friends glided over to the windows of the bridge to see what was happening. Inside, his father was speaking to his uncle, Big Bill, as he was known. He was a huge man and was one of Calron's favourite relatives. He had been one of the first on the scene to help him out during his crash and was the individual who retrieved his downed wind sail for him. He handed his father the comm. speaker, informing him of all details of the emergency.

"They haven't replied to any of our messages and their course has been plotted. They're coming straight at us!"

His father scratched the back of his neck and cleared his throat with an abrupt cough before he switched on the mic.

"This is Dante Udan Lowing of the Zeppelin Cargo Industry. Your flight plan indicates that you are heading on a collision course. Change your coordinates and alter your direction now." He switched off the mic, waiting for a return signal. Nothing.

Again he repeated the message, with frustration now present in his voice.

"Captain! They're slowing down and they've sent a message," the operator informed.

"Show me."

With a few taps of her keyboard the message was displayed as clear as day - *Time to die.*

A frightening explosion rumbled through the zeppelin, shaking the command bridge and knocking over ornaments and computers that smashed and littered the ground.

"Our engines are hit and are now failing! It's the terrorists!" the operator screamed.

Calron suddenly felt completely isolated; he had heard horrific tales about these cults and what they were capable of. A roaring sound began to grow in intensity, chasing away the terrified birds flocked on the top of the zeppelin. Calron and his friends turned to face the sky as the noise became ever louder and more deafening. Sheer horror struck their hearts as the clouds parted and the nose of a terrorist aircraft screamed overhead. Fire was exchanged from both ships and all hell broke loose. Small aircraft started the terrorist assault on the zeppelin, surrounding the massive vessel and cutting off any escape routes, even though it wasn't going far because of the damaged engines. Crewmen brought their rifles up and opened fire on the terrorist aircraft. The mixture of bullets and lasers slammed into the fast descending ships but their armour was too thick. The first ship to land had unexpectedly docked next to one of the few anti-aircraft guns placed on board. Inside, the engineer, Louis, did not hesitate and blew the entire aircraft clean off the dock. But there where more, too many to track and some had already landed on other sections of the landing deck. Lightly armoured troops came running out of the aircraft and, without pausing, shot down four crewmen. Gunfire and explosions could be heard from all corners of the zeppelin. Dante was quick to order a code red emergency to all personnel, instructing the families to head towards the engineering department on the fourth floor. Calron snapped back into action and led his group of friends to the safety of a shelter. Stray fire made their short journey extremely treacherous, so much so that Jim was hit in the arm and lost control of his already damaged wind-sail. Spiralling downwards his beloved wind-sail scraped and scarred the deck below, throwing him clear. He rolled several times before he eventually stopped dead in his tracks. Miraculously he survived the fall and yelled for help. As hazardous as it was, a determined group of friends raced towards him. Bobo picked him up, and with the help of Calron, laid him on the makeshift rear seat of his wind-sail. Nara suffered a shot to her engine which chirred and grinded the bullet until it clogged and rattled uncontrollably. She leapt off and watched it twirl and shake violently, before whizzing off in a random direction and crashing into the ground.

"No!" she screamed, her escape prevented.

Calron dived to her rescue,

"Get on, quick!" he demanded, his heart pounding in his chest.

Leaping onto his back, she flung her arms around his waist and hung on for dear life as the group now fled on half the vehicles they had started off with. Pillars of smoke rose high into the atmosphere, blocking their view and clogging their lungs. Bringing their wind-sails towards the shelter they decreased their altitude, low enough for crewmen on the ground to help them off. Calron's parents were among the new arrivals, the baby screaming madly, never letting her company forget that she was there. His mother tried feverishly to calm her down, but it was the middle of a fire-fight, so not an easy task. Nara still clung onto him so he held her close to reassure her that they were safe. Bobo wasn't letting Jim pass out anytime soon; his solution to repeatedly and encouragingly hit him in the face, preventing him from falling unconscious. Throughout the smoke a single terrorist soldier came running out and opened fire on Calron's family. They ducked for cover as the bullets seared overhead. The terrorist was screaming profanities as he charged at the crewmen. Calron's mother screamed, still clutching onto the baby, as the crewmen returned fire; however, their shots went wide and the terrorist had time to move to a new position, ready to open fire. That was until Big Bill arrived carrying his monstrous sized weapon and took aim. The result - he blew the terrorist bastard clean in two. Smirking, he rested his cannon on his shoulder and helped Dante to his feet.

"Brings back memories of the rebel days," he reminded Dante.

Brings back memories? What the hell is he talking about? Calron wondered. Dante grinned,

"Sure does, old friend."

Calron couldn't believe what he was hearing; his own father a rebel hero - no way! He was an exceptional pilot and a good mechanic, but a rebel? They were just stories his father had told him when he was little, about the rebels who fought against a corrupt government in order to save the zeppelin industry. A sudden shudder rocked the metal ground below and brought back the ominous fear that had left them prematurely.

"Calron!" a familiar voice called, "Calron!"

Calron sat bolt upright and found himself back in the *Alpha One.* He was drenched in sweat and breathing irregularly. Adaman called his name and approached him, his eyes white as snow; he placed a hand on Calron's shoulder and leaned at his side, his voice sounding clear through his re-breather. His suit and amour were immaculate.

"You are troubled?"

Calron slowed his breathing and calmed himself down,

"It was nothing, just a bad dream," he lied, trying to hide the immense pain from the memory of those days.

Standing up he noticed the monitor was off.

"I'm here to let you know the Bigadon infiltrator is on this ship awaiting your meeting."

What? Her! He suddenly found his mind clouded by her image.

"What does she want?" He asked, adjusting his cuffs.

"She wouldn't say – come along now, she waits," he prompted.

Calron nodded and walked alongside Adaman out of the room. He was relieved to be taken away from those memories and tried not to show guilt for concealing them from Adaman. The only problem was that Calron knew that Adaman had already figured out what he was so worked up about, and with good reason... some nagging doubt told him that Adaman was there on that fateful day.

Chapter XXIV
I-Com

The next day Anya awoke confused. She recalled the pickup from her village, followed by the journey to GEMINI. Yes, it was all clear now. Slowly, she lifted her head until she found the ecstatic face of her re-discovered friend Joy, who was leaning over her, grinning.

"Guess who's bunking with you!" she shouted excitedly, as she bounced around the bedroom. It now came back to her that she had been placed with Joy the previous night – they would share a small apartment together – for a while, at least.

She smiled earnestly and lifted her torso from where it had made a warm groove in the soft casing of her new bed. She remembered asking Miss Pince if they could be placed together, at least until the housing plans were made.

"That means we've got the whole place to ourselves! What day's today?"

"Tuesday," Joy replied, and Anya's heart sank. "But don't worry – we don't have to go to lessons until next week – we've been encouraged to explore this place first. They won't start teaching us until all the children are here." She sighed deeply, and lazily dropped her head onto the plush pillow. For a minute she had been worried that Joy was ready and eager to get out – and then noticed she still had her sleep suit on.

Joy dived back onto the bunk above her and quickly pulled the thick covers over her.

"I'm so excited – I can't wait to go sight-seeing! I can't believe that I only met you again yesterday – it feels as if I've know you all my life, despite going our different ways at primary."

Anya yawned in agreement.

"It's lucky that we were put together – I would have hated to be put with the likes of that Pamela girl."

"Oh, she's not that bad," Joy said apprehensively. "I'm sure she's just having trouble adjusting or something."

"I'm hungry." Anya kicked off her covers and pushed the bedroom door open.

"We're not supposed to eat until eight," Joy recalled to her. Anya moaned loudly – all these rules and regulations, obstacles in the way of her being able to make this her new home.

"It's Ok, sleepy head," Joy joked as she shoved her playfully. "Think about it – things could have been a lot worse."

"Well, I may as well get to know our apartment," she added as she tumbled sleepily out of the bedroom and into the kitchen. To the right of the room, in a space of its own, was a high-tech digital HP.

"We should start here," Joy suggested as she pulled over two large leather chairs from the kitchen table and edged them under the holoputer desk.

"Ok. How do we turn this thing on?"

"Didn't you ever do IT in primary? I think this model is one in the range that responds to oral commands. Yep – look there," Anya directed her eyes to a small cluster of oddly shaped triangles printed at the bottom corner of the monitor.

"It doesn't tell me anything. Anyway, let's get it on. Holoputer, on!" she commanded. Nothing happened. An embarrassing silence filled the room, and Joy turned a deep shade of red. Anya chuckled mischievously at her misunderstanding.

"It doesn't work like that." She scanned underneath the cluster of triangles, where there was a code number – 852.

"852," she read out, and the monitor flicked alight.

"Result!" Joy exclaimed, ashamed of her own juvenile attempt.

A status document appeared on-screen and then quickly vanished. Two named icons popped up. One was labelled *Investigative reports,* the other *I-com.*

"Exciting stuff," Anya muttered disappointedly.

"Click on that one."

"This one?" Anya asked. The small communicator pointer attached to her index finger moved the cursor around on the screen, until it fell under Investigative reports,

"No – that looks boring, choose the other one." With a wiggle of her finger Anya selected the icon entitled I-com. Immediately a huge list of references swam onto the screen in waves.

"What's this?" Joy asked confusedly.

"Um – I'm not sure. Let's pick one and see what happens." Anya clicked on the nearest number – room 208. She quickly keyed in a message:

ROOM 852: Hi.

There was a short delay before they received a response.

ROOM 208: Who is this?

ROOM 852: It's Anya and Joy. Who are you?

ROOM 208: I'm Stacey.

"It must be some kind of network," Anya told Joy. "This whole place must be linked by it."

"You could find Albert and Ronald through this, if we knew their room numbers."

"Good idea – but we'll have to wait to the start of next week until we meet them in lessons – there's no hope of finding them outside."

"Hang on," Joy said as she pulled the keyboard out from under Anya's hands.

ROOM 852: Do you know anyone called Albert?

The screen flashed white before a response came up.

ROOM 208: Yes – he's in ROOM 365.

Anya selected the underlined room number and immediately a link was established.

She typed up a greeting.

ROOM 852: Hello? Is Albert or Ronald there?

The holoputer shut off.

"What was that?" Joy asked confused. Anya jabbed with her finger-pointer at the screen, but it remained dead.

"I have no idea. Must have frozen or something." She checked the holoputer's number again, and called it out. It reset automatically, and I-com was brought up instantly.

One of the room icons was flashing red. On closer inspection, it read: LOCKER ROOM.

"What's the matter with this thing now?" Joy asked agitatedly, as she fidgeted around in her cloud-patterned sleep suit.

"Locker room," Anya read. "I don't know – maybe there was a glitch in the network. I'll ask Albert's room." She hastily keyed in a question.

ROOM 852: It's Anya and Joy. Did your holoputer

just shut off?

ROOM 356: Hi Anya and Joy! How are you? It's Ronald here – Albert's still asleep but I'm up fiddling with this holoputer. Sorry – no, nothing happened here.

ROOM 852: We just got cut off. Any idea why?

ROOM 356: Sorry, I can't be of much help. I'm just getting to know how to use this thing.

ROOM 852: That's too bad. Well, we look forward to seeing you two again soon. Sorry, we'd better go and see what the problem is with this thing.

ROOM 356: Ok, no prob, see you later.

Anya closed the conversation window. There it was again, demanding her attention:

- LOCKER ROOM –

Its icon flashed red, and a strange whining noise emitted from the integrated speakers on the side of the monitor.

"Joy, I don't like this – it sounds like the holoputer's distressed."

"More like a cat being strangled if you ask me." Joy also looked concerned. Something was wrong.

A new window darted up to get their attention.

- LOCKER ROOM -
- LOCKER ROOM -

- LOCKER ROOM -
Execute?

"Don't do anything," Joy ordered as she reached for their comtel "I'll see if I can get someone up here." The whining noise grew louder when she lifted the device, until it became almost unbearable. She dropped it to the floor, a look of desperation appearing on her face.

The window on the holoputer continued to flash, casting warm red glows into the kitchen. The minimal lighting they had set on in their apartment cut off. The only source of light remaining was the succession of red bursts from the message on the monitor, which refused to disconnect from the HP.

"Anya, what do we do?!"

Anya could see the whites of her friend's eyes shine under the glow of the flashing message. Her pupils had become small and sharp, and for the first time since they had met she was truly scared. She didn't blame her. She was scared too.

What was happening? Was it something they had done? Her voice croaking with fear, she read the holoputer's ID code and commanded it to turn off. It refused, insisting that she answer this urgent message. She closed her eyes and commanded,

"Execute." The screen went dead and they were left in darkness…

Glossary

A'uran (Ay-uran) – Son of the MageLord.

Adaman Agustas (Adam-an) – A powerful Karmiac who provides guidance to Calron.

Al Ta'un (Al – Ta-une) – Captain of the Fera who battled the OverCast outside the Water Temple.

Albert – Student attending GEMINI, he befriends Anya and Joy.

Alpha One – A small rescue-class ship, belonging to the Alpha Team.

Alpha Team – The renowned rescue team currently working for Captain George C. Band.

Amrak – The opposite of Karma, Amrak is the spiritual energy of degeneration and imbalance which has greatest effect when used to destroy or kill. It can also be used for other purposes by someone with the natural ability to harness it, though it is much rarer to find someone with this ability than those with a talent for using its opposite, Karma.

Anya – A 13 year-old student attending Pharsee's main schooling complex, GEMINI.

Arbus Wrathen (Ar-bus Wrath-en) – The supreme commander of the Gatheren Military, he is a dangerous and confused warrior who has declared war on the Bigadons - a war which has lasted for over a hundred years.

Azul – A Reptan commander.

Bigadons (Big-a-dons) – A friendly race encountered by the humans on Pharsee.

Bryan O'Neil – Arms dealer onboard the Horizon.

C.R.A.P. (Controlled Responsive Assisting Pilot) - Robot pilot for the Alpha Team.

C'kran (See-kran) – Son of the MageLord.

Calron Udan Lowing (Cal-ron) – Commander of the Alpha Team.

Casts – Most commonly found shadow spirit of the OverCast, they are known to attack Feran warriors in their thousands.

Catriona (Kat-rina) – Captain George's daughter.

Cion (Sigh-on) – Murderous machines that have not been in evidence for years.

Coda – Government/military organisation.

Conquest System – A newly discovered galaxy.

Crede – Close colleague of Heme, also accompanies Starna in her explorations.

D'ohk (Dee-ock) – Son of the MageLord.

Dante (Dan-te) - Calron's father.

Dark Sun Clan – Terrorist group.

Delta Team – an elite cadre of soldiers, this team comprises of Alpha, Beta, Gamma, Delta, of which Beta is the only known survivor, who later renames himself Trooper Brown.

Distance – A galactic cruiser.

Dozer – A Dark Sun member who fell victim to the Gatheren.

Dun – A Toxican boss.

Dweb (Dweb) – Leader of the Toxican colony.

Edward Morgue – The chief scientist responsible for John's predicament.

Fera (Fer-a) – an ancient race who once dominated planet Pharsee, they were wiped out by the OverCast in the final showdown on the planet's plains. They are also known as the Pharseeans.

Flare - A galactic cruiser.

Gathera (Gather-ra) – Homeworld to the united colonies of the Gatheren.

Gatheren (Gather-en) – A hostile race equipped with advanced technology and composed of many different races united under the same banner.

Gazra – Chancellor-in-waiting of the entire Bigadon population living on Pharsee.

GEMINI – The largest and best-equipped educational and housing facility for the humans on Pharsee.

General Gargant – The General of the HAF military.

George Cameron Band – Current Captain of the galactic cruiser, the Horizon.

HAF – Human Alliance Forces.

Harro – (Har-row) – A Bigadon home-world.

Heme – An experienced archaeologist who accompanies Starna in her explanation of an ancient Pharseean Temple.

Jake Barrows – John's false ID, given to him by the Captain of the Horizon.

John Spader – Number Five.

Joy – An old friend of Anya's, they were reunited in GEMINI.

Karma – Spiritual energy of life and growth, it can also be used for many different purposes by those with the natural ability to harness it.

Kayla – Calron's mother.

Knarlock (Nar-lock) – More commonly known as Knarlock the Great, he is the leader of the Reptan colony.

L'gis (Ell-gis) – Son of the MageLord.

Logar (Lo-gar) – A human-occupied world.

MPCD Multi-Purpose Combat Droid

MPD Multi-Purpose Droid

MageLord (Mage-lord) – Father of A'uran, C'kran, L'gis and D'ohk, he is the leader of the Fera and resides in the Light Temple on Pharsee.

Miss Pince – A supervisor of the students attending GEMINI.

Mites – creatures of an unspeakable nature; their purpose is unclear, but they have waged an ongoing war with the Gatheren.

Nara, Bobo and Jim – Calron's childhood friends.

Ocorius – (Ocur-ius) – A mite-infested comet, and the location of The Slaughter.

OmniCast (Om-nay-Cast) – Largest of the OverCast, they are almost invincible to attack. When struck, they metamorphose in to creatures more deadly than before.

Oracle – Gatekeeper to the spiritual dimension, also known as The Flux, he is known to favour the appearance of a small snowman.

OverCast (Over-Cast) – A race created from the eerie shadows and rivals of the Fera, both races caused each others total demise in the final showdown on the planet's plains.

Pharsee (Far-see) – A mysterious world.

Plato (Pla-toe) - Logar's moon, and a very useful site for Logar's early warning system.

Portal Dome –Hemispherical structures which allow the Gatheren to teleport from one planet to another.

Private Strome – An undercover operative currently working in the HAF.

Rako – Conquest's sun.

Repta (Rep-ta) – Homeworld of the Reptans.

Reptan (Rep-tan) – Ferocious creatures armed with deadly weapons, they are the most experienced of the Gatheren races in close combat.

Ridley – Leader of the Dark Sun Clan.

Ronald – A friend of Albert.

Seeth – Destroyed world.

Slayer – An MPD owned by the Alpha Team.

Star Lance – A galactic cruiser, destroyed while trying to escape from Earth.

Starna – A female Bigadon infiltrator, trained to undertake missions or investigations that are potentially life-threatening.

Stoke – A Reptan leader.

Tank Mark 2 – An MPCD who was created by the Redura Company, for a purpose which he does not yet know. Now a member of the Alpha Team.

The Cycle of Elements – A group of six Temples: Light, Fire, Shadow, Earth, Water and Wind, positioned on the surface of Pharsee in order to create a cycle of powers central to Feran belief.

The Flux – The grounds of confrontation between the two spiritual powers, Karma and Amrak.

The Great Clam – A devious creature used to provide false information to the Gatheren until it met its end at the wrath of Arbus.

The Marvel – A galactic cruiser.

The Redura Company – An untrustworthy and secretive company.

Torta (Tor-ta) – Homeworld of the Tortans.

Tortan (Tor-tan) – Heavily armoured leviathans, they are dual-purpose - both as shock troops and biological tanks in the Gatheren military.

Toxica (Tox-i-ca) – Homeworld of the Toxicans.

Toxican (Tox-i-can) – The most numerous of the Gatheren races, they are without number and serve as the basic soldiers for the Gatheren.

Trooper Brown – Last known survivor of the Delta Team, who is now a respected member of the Alpha Team.

Turteck (Tur-teck) – Leader of the Tortan colony.

Tyran (Ty-ran) – The largest and most powerful of the Gatherens' many different races; bipedal creatures used in battle as transporters by the Reptans.

Viscounts – The symbolic leaders of the Feran people, they inhabit each of the Temples in The Cycle of Elements.

Zulu – A Reptan leader.

Coming Soon. . .
The Third Millennium
Book II: Further into the Future

Chapter I
Deployment Plans

Standing beside newly promoted Lieutenant Strome, General Gargant watched as the most advanced equipment granted to the HAF was tested on the open training grounds in the Military centre on Logar. The battered ground was covered with a sheet of sand that constantly shifted underneath the Serpent battle tanks as they hovered overhead, casting large elongated shadows back and forth. Down below, the infantry were marching in formed ranks, like a great tide of grey washing over the ground. High above, B19 hunters swooped downwards, dividing the murky clouds before setting targets alight with their ferocious chain-guns and highly explosive scorpion missiles.

Inside the watchtower department of the command centre silence flooded the room, only broken when the General had something to say or to slurp down his KSK Dark.

"Humanity…" the General exhaled, "For as long as we have been in existence so too has war… and it will continue to be so." The General paused to gulp down another mouthful of his coffee.

Bewildered by this unusual remark, Strome added,

"Sometimes, sir, might I add that there can be no alternative."

The General shot Strome a wide-eyed look before turning back to resume overseeing the testing.

"Yes, I agree that it's inevitable. Impressive, isn't it?" he questioned, deliberately changing the subject.

Strome followed his gaze to observe the action taking place outside but did not reply.

A moment of silence passed by as the two watched the full might of the HAF reveal itself. A series of faint explosions rumbled across the plains signifying target practice for the Serpent tanks…

"Lieutenant Strome, what if I was to propose the deployment of Regiment 5 to the newly discovered planet Pharsee?"

The Lieutenant quickly turned back to face the General.

"First of all, sir, I'd ask why?"

The General had anticipated that his proposal would cause confusion in the mind of the Lieutenant, so without further delay he prepared to explain his reasons. Walking over to his seat at the imposing metallic discussion table he punched in a code to his holoputer. Access was confirmed with a subtle beep and the glass panels on the viewing port slowly began to transform into an unfamiliar map. The General strode back to stand side-by-side with Strome, who was already captivated by the sudden change.

The Lieutenant's eyes had been drawn to the enormous pentagonal-shaped segment at the top right corner of the display. Speechless, Strome murmured,

"Sir…is that a-"

"Yes Lieutenant it's a structure alright," the General interrupted, "A bloody big one by the look of things. It's called the Bigadon Plaza and appears to be their home city by all accounts."

The General allowed the Lieutenant a brief moment to come to terms with the sheer size of the structure.

"Aside from our normal military headquarters on the space cruiser Horizon initially sent there, we have also been given permission to set up a small landing site in the southern section of the Plaza. Our old alliance with the Bigadon race has been tested in the last couple of years but it's paid off. They need our help and at a time like this I personally don't want to disappoint them."

"Help with what?" Strome still seemed oblivious to what was going on.

General Gargant relayed in another code, bringing up a highly detailed perspective of the map.

"Red targets indicate several other structures, five in total along with the Plaza itself," he explained carefully.

Strome viewed in turn the five red targets fixated on the map... but on closer inspection there was something else. With another code input the object was clarified as some ship, highlighted in cyan, fish-like in form, a sleek craft and, without question, of epic proportions.

"The Bigadons have sent word for our help... they strongly believe that this is an alien craft belonging to those they have called the 'evil people'."

"More extraterrestrials, sir?" Strome replied, clearly interested in the concept.

"Possibly, but that's why we're leaving for Pharsee in forty-eight hours time. Any questions?" he asked rhetorically.

"No sir."

● ● ●

Returning to his private chamber, Strome quietly sat down and flicked on his holoputer. He briefly checked the news update confirming the deployment to Pharsee in 45 hours time and counting.

Shutting the door he returned to his desk and started a secure channel across to the Redura Network. As expected he was welcomed by the face of his real employer, a grim looking scientist, Dr. Edward Morgue.

"I trust all has gone to plan?"

"We leave for Pharsee in less than two days."

"Good, then you know what to do…and Strome, subject Number Five must be brought back alive, at any cost," he grated icily. "The chassis is almost complete."

Nodding in agreement, Strome closed the connection, shut off his holoputer and left the room…knowing exactly what he had to do.